WHY IS CAROLE PICKING ON HER GUEST?

"Oops," Marie said quietly. Again she adjusted her position in the saddle.

"Okay, that's a little better," Carole said crisply. "Now let's work on the way you're holding the reins. Don't curl your wrists, and keep your thumbs pointing up and your elbows in. And stop twisting around to look at me! You're going to confuse your horse. You've got to keep your eyes looking in the direction you want to go."

Stevie broke that particular rule for a second by twisting around to catch a glimpse of Marie's face. Marie looked harried, and no wonder. Carole barely seemed to pause for breath as she continued to bark out instuctions. The advice she was giving Marie sounded more like plain old criticism, and that wasn't like Carole at all. . . .

THE SADDLE CLUB

RIDING LESSON

BONNIE BRYANT

A SKYLARK BOOK
NEW YORK • TORONTO • LONDON • SYDNEY • AUCKLAND

RL 5, 009-012

RIDING LESSON

A Bantam Skylark Book / September 1994

Skylark Books is a registered trademark of Bantam Books,
a division of Bantam Doubleday Dell Publishing Group, Inc.
Registered in the U.S. Patent and Trademark Office and elsewhere.

"The Saddle Club" is a registered trademark of Bonnie Bryant Hiller.
The Saddle Club design/logo, which consists of a riding crop and a riding
hat, is a trademark of Bantam Books.

"USPC" and "Pony Club" are registered trademarks of The
United States Pony Clubs, Inc., at The Kentucky Horse Park,
4071 Iron Works Pike, Lexington, KY 40511-8462.

ISBN 0-553-48151-7

Published simultaneously in the United States and Canada

Bantam Books are published by Bantam Books, a division of Bantam Doubleday Dell Publishing Group, Inc. Its trademark, consisting of the words
"Bantam Books" and the portrayal of a rooster, is Registered in U.S. Patent
and Trademark Office and in other countries. Marca Registrada. Bantam
Books, 1540 Broadway, New York, New York 10036.

PRINTED IN THE UNITED STATES OF AMERICA

OPM   0 9 8 7 6 5 4

I would like to express my
special thanks to Catherine Hapka
for her help in the writing
of this book.

"NOW *THAT* WAS what I call disgusting," Carole Hanson declared.

"Oh, come on," her father teased. "Didn't you think it was at least a little bit interesting?"

"Yeah, Carole," added Marie Dana. "I thought you were interested in all creatures, great and small."

Carole shot her a dirty look as Colonel Hanson and Marie's mother laughed. "That's the problem," Carole said. "Some of *those* creatures weren't so small!"

The creatures to which Carole was referring were the creepy and crawly inhabitants of the insect zoo, an exhibit at the Smithsonian Institution's Museum of Natural History. The insect zoo featured many varieties of live insects from all over the world. Carole wasn't normally squeamish about such things. But somehow, seeing thousands of insects—some the size of her hand—gathered together in one spot had given her the willies.

"I have to admit, some of those tropical cockroaches did bring back unpleasant memories of places I was stationed before Carole was born," Colonel Hanson said. In his eighteen-year career in the Marine Corps, he had spent time in all kinds of places all over the world. When Carole was younger, her family had moved a lot, but since her mother's death from cancer a couple of years earlier they had lived in Willow Creek, Virginia, a small town about thirty miles outside Washington, D.C.

"Well, if they want some more bees for their collection, they can have the ones that have set up house in my garage," Mrs. Dana said as the foursome strolled through a hallway featuring glass cases filled with skeletons of animals and birds.

"Funny, Mom," Marie said. "Can they have the spiders who've been spinning cobwebs in my bedroom since the last time you vacuumed, too?"

"Ha-ha," said Mrs. Dana dryly in return. "There's no law against daughters vacuuming their own rooms, as far as I know."

"Can't," Marie replied promptly. "I'm still recovering from my injuries. No hard physical labor for me."

Her mother rolled her eyes. Carole couldn't help shaking her head. Sometimes she found Marie's sense of humor a little bizarre. Marie had been in a serious car accident a while ago. The accident had left her in critical condition and had claimed her father's life. Carole had first met Marie when she was still in the hospital, confined to a gurney with a fractured pelvis and two broken legs. Having lost her own mother, Carole could empathize. In fact, she had tried her best to help Marie through the difficult time following Mr. Dana's death.

Colonel Hanson had played a similar role in Mrs. Dana's recovery. He had begun as an understanding friend, and things had slowly developed into something more than friendship. Carole had noticed that her father and Mrs. Dana had been seeing a lot of each other lately.

As if reading Carole's thoughts, Colonel Hanson reached out and took Mrs. Dana's hand in his own. "Don't worry, Olivia," he said with mock seriousness. "If there are any bugs terrorizing you, just let me know. I'll send Carole right over to take care of them."

Now it was Marie's turn to roll her eyes. "Yeah, right," she told Colonel Hanson. "I think the only insect Carole might be interested in seeing would be a fly." She waited for the others' puzzled looks, then grinned. "A *horse*fly, that is."

Colonel Hanson and Mrs. Dana laughed appreciatively at the joke.

Carole spent just about all her free time at Pine Hollow Stables, where she took riding lessons and boarded her horse, Starlight. She had already decided that she would continue to work with horses when she grew up—though whether she would do so as a trainer, breeder, competitive rider, or veterinarian she hadn't yet decided. She had even started a group called The Saddle Club with her best friends, Stevie Lake and Lisa Atwood, who also rode at Pine Hollow. The Saddle Club had only two rules—members had to be horse crazy, and they had to be willing to help each other out.

Carole managed a weak smile in response to Marie's joke. She was a little distracted, and not just by the memories of the spiders and centipedes she'd just seen. She was wondering if there was something more to this outing than there appeared to be. It was a beautiful September Saturday, and Carole had been planning all week to spend the day at Pine Hollow with Lisa and Stevie and Starlight. Starlight was still young, and Carole liked to spend every spare moment on his training. Lately she had started working with him on the half halt, a dressage move in which she asked him for a momentary hesitation in stride. It was a slightly more advanced exercise than Starlight had learned before, and Carole wanted to make sure he was learning it properly.

But a few days earlier Colonel Hanson had announced that he had volunteered to show the Danas around the museums in Washington, and he wanted Carole to come. Carole had been a little disappointed to miss a day of training with her gelding, but she accepted the new plan as cheerfully as she could. She loved visiting the Smithsonian, and she had been so busy with riding and the new school year that she hadn't spent much time with her father lately. By the time she finished her morning riding classes at Pine Hollow, she was actually looking forward to the trip.

Carole was having fun seeing the museums—they had already covered the Air and Space Museum and the National Gallery before heading to the Natural History Museum—but she couldn't help noticing that both her father and Mrs. Dana had been acting a little bit strangely the whole day. She couldn't quite put a finger on what it was about their behavior that bothered her—she just had a feeling that there was something a little eager, almost phony, in their manner. It was making her feel a little edgy, and Marie's sarcastic sense of humor wasn't really helping her mood. Carole glanced at the other girl as they headed for the stairs to the museum's ground floor, wondering if Marie had noticed anything strange about their parents' behavior.

"Anyone for a quick snack?" Colonel Hanson suggested. He patted his belly. "All those bugs made me hungry."

Marie laughed. "Lead the way," she said. "I'm dying for a good wormburger—and maybe some french *flies* on the side."

"Marie, please!" Mrs. Dana exclaimed. She slipped her

arm into Colonel Hanson's as they started down the wide, echoing stairwell. "I *was* hungry, until my charming daughter's comment."

"Maybe they should market you as a diet aid, Marie," Colonel Hanson joked.

Marie smiled proudly. Carole found herself thinking, not for the first time that day, how much livelier and more upbeat Marie seemed these days. The girls hadn't seen each other in several weeks. Marie lived only half a mile from Pine Hollow, and she liked to ride there occasionally. But since school had started, Carole hadn't seen her at the stable.

"Have you been riding lately, Marie?" she asked.

She was a little startled when all three of her companions burst into laughter again.

"Talk about a one-track mind," Marie said. "We were talking about food, remember? Not hay, not oats—people food."

Carole blushed. Sometimes she forgot that everyone else's mind didn't revolve almost constantly around the topic of horses. Still, she found herself wishing—not for the first time that day—that Marie was a little less blunt in her comments.

"Come on, honey," Colonel Hanson said, not seeming to notice Carole's consternation. "I'll buy you a slice of pie or something."

"I'm not really that hungry," Carole muttered, trailing

along behind the others as they walked toward the museum's cafeteria. They passed the large gift shop, dodging a group of excited children waving their brand-new stuffed dinosaurs. The cafeteria featured a revolving selection of snacks and sandwiches. Carole and the others picked up trays and took their places in front of the slowly circling food.

"Hey, Carole, want to share an order of fries?" Marie said, grabbing a large bag of french fries.

Carole shrugged. "Sure. Sounds good." She noticed her father glancing at Mrs. Dana and winking. More than ever she had the feeling that there was something going on. What was more, she was beginning to think she might know what it was, and she wasn't sure she liked her theory. She decided not to think about it.

Soon all four of them had chosen the food and drinks they wanted. Colonel Hanson paid the cashier, and then they managed to find an empty booth in the crowded seating area. As they all ate and chatted about the exhibits they'd seen that day, Carole's mind kept wandering back to her thoughts about her father and Mrs. Dana. Since not thinking about it wasn't working, Carole decided to try looking at things logically, the way Lisa—a straight-A student and the most practical and logical member of The Saddle Club—would.

First, Carole considered the facts. Her father and Marie's mother had been dating for a while now. In the past two weeks they had had dinner together two or three times and had gone to a play and a concert. Now here they were, not only spending more time together, but also making sure that Carole and Marie spent time together. And judging by the looks they kept giving each other, the adults were definitely paying attention to how the girls were getting along.

It all pointed to one thing as far as Carole was concerned. Their parents wanted them to get along because they thought Carole and Marie would be spending a lot of time together soon. Carole scooped up some ketchup on the end of a french fry, ignoring the bug-oriented conversation going on around her. Try as she might, she could think of only one explanation for the adults' behavior. She glanced at her father, then at Mrs. Dana. Then Carole popped the french fry into her mouth and chewed it slowly and thoughtfully.

CAROLE MANAGED TO keep her thoughts to herself until the two families had parted ways and headed to their separate cars for the ride back to Willow Creek.

"All right, what was that all about?" she finally asked as she and her father strolled across the Mall, the large green lawn around which the museums of the Smithsonian were clustered. At one end the tall, thin spire of the Washington Monument stretched toward the sky, while the domed Capitol Building was visible at the other end.

"What was what?" Colonel Hanson asked. He paused

8

briefly to snap a picture of the monument with his instant camera. "The car's right over there," he added, hurrying ahead to unlock the doors.

Carole climbed into the passenger seat and slammed the door shut a little harder than strictly necessary. "What were you and Mrs. Dana winking and smiling about all day?" she demanded as her father got in across from her. "Is there something you're not telling me?"

"Whoa! I surrender!" Colonel Hanson exclaimed, holding up his hands. "I didn't realize we were being that obvious." He started the car and carefully pulled out into the busy late-afternoon traffic.

Carole just crossed her arms and waited.

"Actually, I was going to tell you the news on the way home if things went well today," Colonel Hanson said. "But Olivia and I wanted to watch you and Marie together first to see how you got along before we broke it to you."

Carole took a deep breath. "I think I know what's coming, Dad. And I want you to know that I could probably get used to having Marie as a sister. I mean, I don't really know her that well yet, but as long as you and Mrs. Dana are happy together, that's what—"

"Time out!" Colonel Hanson interrupted. "What are you talking about?"

"Well, aren't you about to tell me you and Mrs. Dana are getting married?"

Colonel Hanson opened his mouth to reply, then turned to stare at her in surprise. When he turned his attention back to the road a second later, he began to laugh. "No, my dear, I'm not!" he said at last. "Oh, honey, I'm sorry to laugh, but you caught me off guard. I can't believe you're in such a hurry to marry me and Olivia off! After all, she lost her husband only a few months ago."

Carole stared at her father. "What were you going to tell me, then?"

"Well, I don't know, it may seem sort of anticlimactic now," Colonel Hanson said teasingly. Carole glared at him, and he relented. "All right, sorry. The truth is, Olivia has to go to Europe on business for a couple of weeks. She can't take Marie with her, obviously, because of school, and she was worried about leaving her alone or with total strangers." He braked for a red light and turned to smile at Carole. "So I invited Marie to stay with us while her mother is away."

"Oh," Carole said, feeling a little relieved. She liked Mrs. Dana a lot, and she definitely wanted her father to be happy, but she didn't think she was quite ready to welcome someone else into their home—not yet. "So that's why you wanted to make sure Marie and I were getting along today."

"Right," her father replied.

Carole gazed out the window as the light changed and the car continued down the street through the busy city traffic. "It could be fun having Marie stay with us," she said after a moment. "She'll be like a temporary sister."

"That's right," Colonel Hanson said. "I'm glad you feel that way. And I'm sure I don't need to tell you that Marie still needs extra compassion from us. It will be difficult for her to be apart from her mother so soon after the accident, even if it's only for a couple of weeks."

"Don't worry," Carole assured him. "I'll be extra nice. Stevie and Lisa will, too." The more she thought about it, the better the plan sounded. Carole had always wondered what it would be like to have a brother or sister, and this would be the perfect chance to find out. Stevie complained about her three brothers almost constantly, but Carole was sure a sister would be different. A sister would be like a good friend, but better, because she would be there all the time.

"Good," Colonel Hanson said. "I'm sure she'll appreciate it. Oh, and I almost forgot to tell you, Marie's birthday is coming up, too. So that's just one more thing we'll have to help her through. Not only will this be her first birthday without her father, but her mother won't be with her either."

Carole nodded. "That'll be tough for her," she said sympathetically. "We'll have to plan something really special for her so she won't miss them both so much."

Colonel Hanson glanced at her again and smiled proudly. "I knew you'd feel that way," he told her. "You've been such a good friend to Marie. And I'm sure you'll be an even better temporary sister."

Carole smiled back. "I'm sure of it, too."

AS SOON AS she got home, Carole hurried to the phone and dialed Stevie's number. "Guess what," she blurted out as soon as Stevie answered.

Stevie laughed. "You sound like me," she said. Stevie was notorious for launching right into conversations without bothering to identify herself.

"Never mind that," Carole said. "I have big news. I'm getting a sister. Well, sort of."

"What?" Stevie yelped. "What do you mean?"

"It's Marie," Carole explained. She quickly filled Stevie in on the news.

"That's terrific," Stevie said when Carole had finished. "I like Marie. She's funny."

"She sure is," Carole replied ruefully, remembering the barrage of bug jokes that afternoon. "Anyway, we should start thinking of lots of things to do while she's staying here."

"Cool," Stevie said. "Why don't we get Lisa in on this, too?"

"Good idea," Carole agreed. "Three-way calling is a great invention, isn't it?"

A moment later Lisa was on the line, too. Carole quickly told her about Marie's visit. "Now we have to think of special things to do for her while she's here. We don't want to give her a spare second to miss her mom."

"What have you thought of so far?" Lisa asked.

"Well, just that we'll want to spend a lot of time at Pine Hollow," Carole said. "I was hoping you guys could help me with the details."

"No problem," said Stevie. "Let's see, we can start with lots of trail rides, maybe a nice autumn picnic in the woods. . . ."

"That all sounds great," Lisa said. "But you're forgetting one very important thing. Sleepovers."

"Oh, well, I guess that goes without saying," Carole replied.

"I guess it does," Lisa said. "But I have an even better idea. Let's ask Max if we can have a sleepover in the stable."

"The stable?" Carole repeated. "You want us to bed down in one of the box stalls?"

Lisa laughed. "Of course not. We can sleep in the loft."

"What a perfect idea!" Stevie exclaimed. "Why didn't I think of that?"

"I guess it does sound kind of like a Stevie plan, doesn't it?" Lisa said. "Although it could just as easily be a Carole plan. After all, you already spend every waking moment at Pine Hollow. I'm surprised it's never occurred to you to spend every *sleeping* moment there, too."

Carole and Stevie laughed.

13

"We must be rubbing off on you," Stevie told Lisa.

"I think you are," Lisa agreed. "And I'm glad. That's what friends are for, right?"

"Right," Carole and Stevie said in one voice.

Carole thought for a moment. "And you know, I think we should all try to be really good friends to Marie while her mother is away," she said. "It will be hard for her, especially on her birthday."

"Sounds like a Saddle Club project to me," Lisa said.

"Definitely," Carole replied wholeheartedly.

CAROLE WATCHED CRITICALLY as Lisa and Prancer walked in a figure eight in the outdoor ring at Pine Hollow the following Thursday afternoon. "I think you're ready to take her to a trot," she called from her position atop Starlight.

Lisa nodded quickly and gave the signal by squeezing gently with both legs and allowing the horse a little more rein. Prancer responded instantly, moving into a smooth trot while continuing in the figure eight as directed. Lisa smiled with pleasure, and Carole nodded with satisfaction as she watched.

Prancer had been a racehorse for the first three years of her life, until a leg injury had ended her racing career. Since the injury had revealed a hereditary weakness, it made her unsuitable as a brood mare for a racing stable despite her impeccable bloodlines. Prancer had a sweet disposition and a love of young people, so Max Regnery, the owner of Pine Hollow, and Judy Barker, the local veterinarian, had decided to buy the mare as a riding horse for the stable.

Once the horse's leg had healed, Lisa had begun to work on training Prancer to be a pleasure mount. As a racehorse she had been taught to do only one thing, and that was race. Part of what the mare needed to learn first was obedience and precision, and that was what Lisa and Carole were teaching Prancer today by putting her through some basic dressage training exercises.

After a few minutes Lisa brought Prancer back to a walk, then to a stop. The mare obeyed perfectly.

"She looks good!" Carole called.

"She feels good, too," Lisa said with a smile. She loved riding the beautiful bay mare, even though the task of training her was painstaking and sometimes tedious. A lot of patient work had preceded today's performance, and Lisa was proud of the results. It was a compliment to her own riding skills that Max was allowing her to work with the mare at this stage. Even though Lisa hadn't been riding as long as her friends had, she had learned very quickly, and Max was confident that she could handle this challenge—especially since Prancer had developed a real affection for her.

"What now?" Lisa asked. Carole knew a lot about train-

16

ing, and Lisa trusted her opinions. She had the feeling Max did, too, and that that was part of the reason he trusted Lisa to work with Prancer. He knew that The Saddle Club always worked as a team.

Before Carole could answer Lisa's question, they both heard Stevie's voice. "Hi, guys! Sorry I'm late! I'll be right out."

With that their friend disappeared into the stable. She reappeared a few minutes later leading Topside, the Thoroughbred gelding she usually rode.

By this time Carole and Lisa had moved ahead with their exercises. They were riding the two horses in a wide circle around the ring with Starlight in the lead. Every so often Carole would ask Starlight to switch from a walk to a trot. Prancer's natural instinct was to move into a trot as well, but Lisa held her to a walk. She was teaching the horse to respond only to what her rider was telling her to do, not to anything that was happening around her. It was an important lesson, and Prancer was getting better at it every day, although she still sometimes became impatient when she felt she was being left behind. Horses are naturally competitive creatures, and Prancer had been bred and trained to race—and win.

"What happened to you?" Carole asked when Stevie and Topside joined them in the ring. She brought Starlight to a halt.

"I kind of lost track of the time," Stevie explained. "See,

there's this new girl in my class at school, Priscilla Tyler. I volunteered to fill her in on some stuff about Fenton Hall." That was the private school Stevie attended, located across town from the public school where Carole and Lisa went. "We got to talking and, well . . ."

"We know," Lisa said. Carole nodded. They knew that when Stevie got to talking, it was sometimes difficult to get her to stop.

"So what'd I miss?" Stevie asked.

Carole quickly explained what they'd been doing. Then they got back to work. At one time Lisa might have thought that doing so much riding at a slow walk would be boring. But when she was involved in teaching a wonderful horse like Prancer something important, as she was now, she didn't mind it at all. All of the mare's gaits were so smooth and pleasant to ride that it almost didn't matter whether she was walking, trotting, cantering, or galloping. Lisa loved riding her at any speed.

After a while Lisa caught a glimpse of movement out of the corner of her eye. She glanced over at the edge of the ring. "Looks like we have company," she called to Carole and Stevie.

Carole turned to see Judy Barker leaning on the gate of the ring. Max and his fiancée, Deborah Hale, were with her. Max and Deborah, a newspaper reporter from Washington, had become engaged recently. The two had met

18

when Deborah had interviewed Max to gather background information for a story about horses.

"Let's go say hello," Carole said eagerly, dismounting and heading toward the gate. Carole had spent some time after school and during vacations assisting Judy on her rounds. It seemed that she learned something new every time she talked to the vet.

"I think Prancer has had just about enough for today anyway," Lisa said. She gave the mare a pat on the neck, dismounted, and followed Carole. Stevie was right behind her.

"Hi, girls," said Judy. "You're looking good out there."

"Prancer is the one who's looking good," Carole said. "She's really a fast learner."

"She's smart," Judy said with a nod. "And you girls are good trainers."

Carole and Lisa blushed with pleasure. But Stevie had things other than compliments on her mind. "Are you here to check on Spice?" she asked Judy excitedly. "Is she going to foal soon?" Spice was a pregnant mare who was staying at Pine Hollow until she foaled. After that she would immediately be bred to Max's stallion, Geronimo.

Judy nodded again. "I already saw her. And as I told Max, I think his estimate is off the mark—I'd say she won't drop the foal for another three weeks at least." Stevie, Carole, and Lisa knew that Max had thought Spice would foal within the next week.

19

"Oh, that's too bad," Stevie said. "You'll love seeing the foal," she added to Deborah, who hadn't spent much time around horses before meeting Max. "They're so cute when they're little."

"But, Max, that means you'll have to keep Spice here a lot longer than you'd planned," Carole said.

Max shrugged. "As I told Judy, it's no big deal. I already agreed to look after the mare. I'll just keep her here until she foals, even if it takes a little longer than I had expected." He smiled at Deborah.

"I can't wait to see the baby," Deborah said cheerfully. She hoisted herself up and perched on the fence. "I've never seen a newborn horse before."

Carole smiled at her. "You'll love it," she said. "Newborn foals are so adorable. I've seen lots of them, especially since I started working with Judy, but each time it's wonderful all over again. It really kind of reminds you somehow what life is all about, you know?"

Deborah nodded, swinging one booted foot against the fence rail. Carole stifled a giggle as she thought how much Deborah's style of dress had already changed since she'd become engaged to Max and started spending a lot of time at Pine Hollow. Today she was wearing blue jeans almost as faded as Stevie's, a plaid flannel shirt, and riding boots. Her shoulder-length red hair was pulled back into a ponytail.

Carole glanced at Max and noticed for the first time that his appearance had changed a little since meeting Deborah, too. He had always dressed neatly and practically, and he still did, but today he was wearing a new shirt that looked more stylish than the ones he usually wore.

Carole looked down at her own dusty riding clothes. I hope getting married doesn't mean you have to change the way you look, she thought. Carole liked to dress up once in a while, especially when she was going to be seeing Cam Nelson, a boy she was friends with. Still, she didn't think she would ever change the way she dressed just to please another person—even Cam.

Her attention snapped back to the conversation with Max's next words. "We've been out looking at china patterns," he said, beaming at Deborah.

"That's right," the reporter added. "We've got it narrowed down to three or four choices."

When the adults weren't looking, Stevie caught Carole's eye and made a gagging face. Carole giggled. The Saddle Club was delighted about Max's upcoming marriage, and they liked Deborah a lot, but sometimes the two of them could get a little carried away. Besides, it was funny to see some of the changes in Max. He normally wasn't the type of person to spend any time at all thinking about something as boring as china patterns.

"I was at the mall with my mother last week," Lisa chimed in, "and we were in the china department of one store because she was buying a wedding gift for someone.

21

They had this great china with fox-hunting scenes on it. You guys could get that."

"Hey, that sounds great," Carole said.

But Max, Deborah, and Judy were laughing.

"I don't think so, Carole," Max said. "We're looking for something that will coordinate well with the dining room. Deborah's got some terrific decorating ideas." He smiled proudly at his fiancée. Her face glowed. Stevie pretended to gag again, and this time Carole was pretty sure Judy saw her. Luckily, though, Max and Deborah had eyes only for each other and didn't notice a thing.

"Speaking of dishes, I'm starved," Deborah said. "I think I'll go over to the house and get a snack." She began to push herself forward off the fence.

"Here, let me help you," Max said. He reached up and took her by the waist, gently lowering her the few feet to the ground.

Deborah smiled at him and gave him a quick kiss on the cheek. "Thanks," she said. "Want to join me?"

"Sorry," Max said with real regret in his voice. "I can't right now. I want to have Judy look in at Bluegrass while she's here. I just want to make sure he's completely over his cold. It will only take a few minutes. I'll join you after that, okay?"

"If you're only going to be a few minutes, I can wait," Deborah said. "Maybe the girls will let me help them take off—oh, I mean *untack* their horses."

"You're learning the lingo," Max said. "All right, then. If you don't mind waiting, I'll be back in a jiffy."

As Max and Judy headed into the stable, Stevie turned to Deborah, her hands on her hips. "What's the big idea?" she demanded.

Deborah looked startled. She hadn't known Stevie very long and still wasn't quite used to her bluntness. But she recovered quickly like the unflappable reporter she was. "What's what big idea?"

Stevie threw up her hands in exasperation. "You and Max! I mean, you're two of the most independent, plain-spoken people I know. And here you are, treating each other like—like—like that *china* you were talking about!"

"What do you mean?" Deborah asked, with just a hint of a smile. She reached forward gingerly to pat Starlight on the nose. He snuffled at her curiously, then lowered his head for more petting.

"I mean like letting Max help you down from that fence, as if you'd break your legs if you tried to jump down yourself," Stevie said.

Deborah laughed. "Oh, that," she said. "You probably don't want to hear this, but I sometimes let him open doors for me, too."

"But what's the point of all that?" Carole asked. She wouldn't have dared bring up this subject herself, but she was glad that Stevie had. "You're not helpless. You can

23

open doors and get down from fences yourself. Why pretend that you can't?"

"I'm not pretending I can't," Deborah explained. "And Max knows very well that I can do those things myself. He just wants to pamper me a little bit."

Stevie and Carole still looked skeptical. But Lisa was nodding. "I think that's nice," she said. "My dad still does things like that for my mom. It's really sweet."

"It *is* sweet," Deborah agreed. "It makes Max feel good to do those things, and it makes me feel good to let him."

"But isn't that a little, well . . ." Carole glanced down at Starlight's reins as she searched her mind for a tactful word.

"Prehistoric?" Stevie finished helpfully.

Deborah laughed again. "I like to think not. After all, I do little things to pamper Max right back."

Something else was still bothering Carole. "Well, all right, but what about the food thing?" she said. "You're hungry, but you're not going right inside to eat because Max isn't ready yet. What do you call that?"

"I call it compromise," Deborah replied. "Sure I'm hungry, but eating with Max will be much more pleasant for me than eating alone. And I know that he feels the same way. So I'll wait a few minutes and make us both happy."

"Hmm," Stevie said, still looking unconvinced. Carole agreed with the sentiment. It sounded to her as though Deborah was putting Max's needs ahead of her own.

"Well, think about this," Deborah said. "Do you think Max actually *likes* spending his Sunday morning shopping for china patterns?"

The three girls exchanged glances. "No," they answered in one voice.

"But he certainly seemed pretty happy about it today," Carole added.

"I guess it's because you guys were doing it together," Lisa said.

"Barf," said Stevie.

The others laughed. "Come on, Stevie," said Lisa. "It's not like you never act differently around Phil." Phil Marsten was a boy Stevie had met at riding camp. They had been dating ever since, even though he lived in a different town and they could see each other only once or twice a month.

"That's different," Stevie replied with a sniff. "I'm only nice to him when I feel like it."

"Right," Lisa joked. "And you just happen to feel like it almost every single time you see him."

"That's right," Stevie said with a shrug. "What about it?"

"Sounds like true love to me," Deborah said with a wink at Lisa.

While Lisa and Deborah continued to tease Stevie, Carole's mind began to wander again as she thought about what Deborah had said. She thought about the way her father acted with Mrs. Dana. She remembered that he did often open doors or pull out chairs for her—just as he had done for Carole's mother when she was alive. But had he changed in other ways since they'd been dating? Carole didn't think he had, but she hated the thought that he might if things got more serious between them. For instance, Carole knew that Mrs. Dana was very interested in antique furniture. If she married Colonel Hanson and moved in, would she insist on redecorating the house? Carole tried to picture her cozy room filled with dusty old mahogany furniture. She wrinkled her nose at the thought.

Before she could ponder these questions any further, Starlight turned his attention from Deborah back to Carole. He nudged her gently on the shoulder and stamped one foot. "Oh, sorry, boy," Carole said, giving her horse a quick hug. "You guys had such a good training session, and here we are standing around talking instead of giving you a good grooming and letting you rest in your stalls."

"Oh, you're right, Carole," Stevie said, interrupting yet another of Lisa's jokes about Phil. "Come on, Deborah. You can help me with Topside."

As Carole led Starlight into the stable, she decided that she wasn't giving her father enough credit. He was who he was, and that wasn't going to change—even if he did wind up marrying Mrs. Dana.

STEVIE GROANED AS she stacked one book on top of another. It was Monday afternoon, and classes at Fenton Hall had just ended for the day. And it was a good thing, too, Stevie thought. If she had been assigned any more homework, she would have had to hire a moving van to get her books home. If the teachers were already assigning this much work in September, she wasn't sure she wanted to be around for May and June.

With some difficulty she gathered up the tall pile of books and notebooks and staggered away from her locker toward the front doors. She was supposed to meet Priscilla outside. One thing she'd have to be sure to warn her about Fenton Hall was the workload—if she hadn't already figured it out herself.

"Oh, Stevie! There you are!" Priscilla called brightly, hurrying over as Stevie emerged, blinking, into the bright afternoon sunlight. "Here, let me carry some of those for you."

Priscilla reached out, took a few books off Stevie's pile, and stuck them under her arm. She herself was carrying only a small leather satchel slung over one shoulder. It looked more like a fashion accessory to Stevie than a book bag, and she grumpily told Priscilla so.

Priscilla laughed cheerfully and agreed, tossing her long, curly brown hair over one shoulder. "Actually, you're right. I bought it to match these shoes. Aren't they cool?" She held out one foot so Stevie could inspect her stylish dark-brown leather shoes. "I guess I'm lucky," Priscilla continued. "My teachers don't seem to assign much homework, and I've got a study hall last period so I can finish most of it then. I only had to bring one book home today." She patted her bag. "And luckily it's a small one."

Stevie frowned. "Maybe I should transfer into more of your classes," she said. The two girls had only three classes together.

"Oh, I only wish you could!" Priscilla exclaimed. "I mean, the other kids are nice and everything, but, well, it would be nice to have a real friend around, you know?"

"Sure," Stevie said, her mood improving a little. It was nice that Priscilla thought of her as a friend after such a short time. Even though she couldn't have asked for better friends than Carole and Lisa, Stevie sometimes found herself thinking they'd be even more perfect if they went to her school. Stevie was popular with her classmates at Fenton Hall, but she wasn't particularly close to any of them. Maybe Priscilla would be different. Stevie shifted her lightened stack of books to her other arm. "Anyway, I'm supposed to meet my friends Carole and Lisa at TD's now. Do you want to come along and meet them?"

"Okay," Priscilla said agreeably. "Let's go."

The two girls started walking toward the small shopping center where TD's was located. As they walked, Stevie began to tell Priscilla about Prancer's latest training session. The girls had spent most of the weekend at Pine Hollow working with the mare.

"It's just totally amazing to watch her," Stevie said. "I mean, she was trained her whole life just to do one thing—run. Now we're asking her to learn a whole new set of rules and do things she's never had to do before. It took her a while to understand what was going on, but now she's really catching on."

"Uh-huh," Priscilla said.

"Prancer is lucky she's got Carole helping to train her," Stevie continued. "Carole—she's one of the friends we're going to meet, by the way—is really good. She's been training her own horse, Starlight, ever since she got him. She might even be a professional trainer when she grows up."

"Oh, really?" Priscilla said. "When I grow up, I might want to be a fashion designer, or maybe a dancer." She smoothed back her hair. "What do you think?"

"Well, both of those things sound okay, I guess," Stevie said, still thinking about Prancer and Carole.

"Did I tell you that my art teacher said my fashion drawings look really good?" Priscilla went on. "Almost professional, he said."

"That's great," Stevie said. "Do you just draw clothes, or other things, too?"

"Oh, all kinds of things," Priscilla answered. "I took an oil-painting class at the community center in my old town, and we painted fruit and flowers and stuff like that. I've also taken some sketch classes. Maybe you could come over to my house and look at some of my sketches sometime."

"Sure. Did you ever do any pictures of horses?" Stevie asked. "Maybe you could come to Pine Hollow and do some sketches there. The horse I ride, Topside, is really pretty. He's a Thoroughbred, just like Prancer, and he used to compete in big horse shows."

Priscilla shrugged. "I've never drawn horses. I'm really more interested in fashion sketching than anything else."

"Oh." Stevie couldn't muster up much enthusiasm about fashion—it was one topic she rarely spent any time thinking about. She decided to try to switch the topic back to horses again. If she could get Priscilla interested enough, maybe she'd want to start riding at Pine Hollow. That would be just about perfect. Then she would not only have a new friend at school, but she'd be able to share her with her friends at Pine Hollow.

Before Stevie could say anything, though, she felt Priscilla tugging on her sleeve. "Stevie, did you hear what I just asked you?" Priscilla asked plaintively.

"Oh, sorry," Stevie said quickly. "I was, uh, thinking about something for a second. What did you say?"

"I asked you whether you thought this shade of blue looks good with my coloring," Priscilla said, straightening the collar of the powder-blue blouse she was wearing.

"Your what?" Stevie asked.

"My coloring," Priscilla repeated. Seeing the blank look on Stevie's face, she added, "You know, the color of my hair and eyes and my skin tone."

Stevie shrugged. As far as she was concerned, blue was blue, and anybody looked good in it. But she decided to humor Priscilla. "Sure. It looks really great," she said.

Priscilla smiled. "Thanks," she said. "When you didn't answer at first, I thought it meant you didn't like it."

"Nope. It's great," Stevie said. "I love it."

Priscilla seemed satisfied by that, and Stevie decided she'd wait to bring up the topic of horses again when they met Carole and Lisa. After all, it was the one topic that was guaranteed to come up whenever The Saddle Club got together. She and Priscilla chatted about teachers and classes for the rest of the walk.

"Is this the mall?" Priscilla asked as they reached the shopping center where TD's was located. She looked a little disappointed.

"Not exactly," Stevie replied. "There's a larger one—the West End Mall—outside of town."

"Thank goodness!" Priscilla said, shaking her head as she surveyed the stores. "For a second I thought I was going to have to do all my shopping in Washington! Maybe you and I could go to the other mall sometimes. You could show me where all the cool stores are."

Stevie looked around, too. The shopping center was small, she had to admit. Aside from TD's, there was a supermarket, an electronics store, The Saddlery tack shop, and a few other stores. It was nothing fancy, but Stevie liked it. "I guess we could go there sometime," she said. "I'm not really sure I know where all the cool stores are, though. I don't really do that much shopping."

Priscilla smiled. "We'll find them together, then," she said. "I love shopping. It'll be fun."

By this time they had reached TD's. "Come on, let's go in," Stevie said. "Carole and Lisa are probably here already."

She headed into the ice-cream parlor with Priscilla right behind her.

"Stevie!" Carole's familiar voice called. "Over here!"

A moment later Stevie and Priscilla were seated in a booth with Carole and Lisa, and the necessary introductions had been made. "So, Priscilla," Carole said. "Do you ride?"

"No," Priscilla said. She turned to Stevie. "What kinds of ice cream do they have here?" she asked.

"All kinds," Stevie said.

Lisa laughed. "And be forewarned, Stevie likes to eat them all together in one sundae," she said jokingly. Stevie was well-known for the preposterous ice-cream concoctions she always ordered.

The waitress approached the table. She rolled her eyes as she recognized Stevie. Stevie grinned at her. "What'll it be?" the waitress asked resignedly.

"I'll have chocolate ice cream with marshmallow topping," Carole decided.

"Oh, that sounds good," Lisa said. "I'll have the same."

"And for you?" the waitress asked, turning to Priscilla.

"Nothing for me, thanks," Priscilla said. She patted her slender stomach. "I'm on a diet."

The waitress looked at Stevie with a hopeful smile. "You're not on a diet, too, are you?"

Stevie smiled back. "I'm afraid not," she said. "In fact, I'm feeling hungrier than usual today. I think I'll have a banana split."

The waitress jotted it down, looking relieved. She turned to go.

"Just a second," Stevie said. "I want to make a few minor alterations."

"Why doesn't that surprise me?" the waitress said sarcastically, turning back to Stevie with a sigh.

"Instead of the vanilla and strawberry ice cream, I'd like to have bubble gum and pistachio. And could you substitute the chocolate syrup with peppermint topping and throw in some peanut-butter chips? And go heavy on the pineapple topping."

The waitress wrote it all down, her jaw set. Then she turned on her heel and left without another word.

"Her disposition just gets worse and worse every time we come in here," Stevie said innocently. "It must be the stress of the job."

Lisa and Carole laughed. Priscilla looked a little confused by the exchange, but The Saddle Club didn't give her time to worry about it.

"So, Priscilla," Lisa said. "You go to Fenton Hall with Stevie, right?"

"That's right," Priscilla said. "It's wonderful there, especially with Stevie showing me around. She seems to know everybody."

"That's our Stevie," Carole agreed as Stevie grinned proudly. "She knows everyone, and everyone knows her. Max likes to say that when Stevie first started coming to Pine Hollow, she knew everyone there—horses *and* people —within the first week!"

"Max?" Priscilla repeated. "Is that your boyfriend, Stevie?"

Carole and Lisa burst out laughing. "Don't let Deborah hear about this, Stevie," Lisa teased. "Or Phil, for that matter."

Stevie chuckled, too, but seeing that Priscilla looked a little disconcerted, she quickly explained who Max was and why they were laughing.

Then the talk turned to horses, as The Saddle Club began to discuss once again the progress Prancer was making.

"I think that if she keeps doing as well as she's been doing this week, we should ask Max if we should start working on collection soon," Carole commented.

Stevie turned to Priscilla. " 'Collection' is a dressage term," she explained. "It's when a horse's center of gravity is over its hindquarters, so it looks like its strides are shorter and its whole body is more compact. It makes it easier for the horse to respond instantly to its rider's signals."

"Hmm," Priscilla said, taking a sip of water.

Stevie didn't think that qualified as a very enthusiastic response. She wondered if the term was too hard for a beginner to understand.

"Anyway, it's really interesting to work with another horse after training Starlight for so long," Carole was saying. "It gives me a new perspective on things he's done and things he could be doing."

"I just think it's wonderful that Prancer is doing so

35

well," Lisa said. "She's come such a long way in such a short time." At one time Lisa hadn't realized how far Prancer had to go in her training. She had even tried to ride the mare in a horse show, realizing only after the fact that Prancer wasn't anywhere near ready for competition. Because of that mistake Lisa now took Prancer's training very seriously. She welcomed any chance to discuss it, and Carole and Stevie were always happy to oblige.

In fact, the only person at the table who didn't look happy to be discussing Prancer's training was Priscilla. Stevie continued to explain what they were talking about, hoping to spark the girl's interest, but it didn't seem to be working. Priscilla alternated between staring blankly into space and playing with her straw.

The conversation was interrupted by the arrival of the waitress with their ice cream. "Enjoy," she said dryly as she placed the heaping banana split in front of Stevie.

"Thanks. I will," Stevie said, licking her lips in anticipation. She picked up her spoon, then paused. "Would anyone like a taste?"

Carole and Lisa, their mouths already full of their own ice cream, shook their heads. They liked to say that one reason Stevie always ordered such unusual sundaes was because she didn't want to have to share them. Still, they had to admit that she always offered politely.

"I'll try a little taste," Priscilla said, picking up a spoon.

Stevie's jaw dropped. Carole and Lisa almost choked on

their ice cream. "Really?" Stevie said. "Oh, uh, I mean, go ahead. Take as much as you want." She slowly slid the dish across the table toward Priscilla.

Priscilla daintily gathered a bite of chocolate ice cream, peanut-butter chips, and peppermint and pineapple toppings onto her spoon. As the other three girls stared in amazement, she popped the spoon into her mouth, chewed, swallowed, and smiled. "Mmm. Good choice, Stevie," she said. "Thank you for the taste."

Stevie gulped. "Y-you're welcome." She pulled the dish back and stared at it. It was a rare day that Stevie Lake was speechless, but she was speechless now.

Carole wisely decided to change the subject. "Stevie, before you got here, Lisa and I were saying we should ask Max soon about using the hayloft in the stable."

"Carole's friend Marie is going to be staying with her for a couple of weeks, and we're having a sleepover for her this Saturday night in the loft at Pine Hollow," Lisa explained to Priscilla. "That is, we're having it in the loft if Max will let us." She turned to Stevie. "Since you're so good at talking people into things, why don't you mention it to him?"

"But it was your idea," Stevie protested, finally recovering from her shock enough to pick up her spoon and start to eat.

"I'm with Lisa," Carole said. "Stevie, you're the genius

at convincing people to do things they don't really want to do."

"Why would you want to sleep in a stable, anyway?" Priscilla put in.

Carole shrugged. "Just for fun."

"Well, it sounds like a pretty smelly kind of fun to me," Priscilla said with distaste. She stood up and gathered her things together. "Stevie, I've got to get going. I'll see you tomorrow at school. We're going to sit together at lunch, right?"

"Sure," Stevie said. "See you then."

"Good-bye, Priscilla. It was nice to meet you," Lisa said politely.

"I'm sure we'll see you again soon," Carole added.

" 'Bye," Priscilla said, slinging her leather bag over her shoulder. "Nice to meet you, too."

When she had gone, the talk returned to Marie's upcoming visit. "When is she arriving?" Lisa asked Carole.

"Tomorrow after school," Carole replied.

"It'll be neat to have her staying with you for two whole weeks," Lisa said, sounding a little envious. "Having a sister must be wonderful."

"I'll say," Stevie put in. "Maybe we could work out some kind of a trade—you know, Marie could come stay with me, and my brothers could move into your house."

"No deal," Carole said with a laugh. "I'm sure having Marie for a temporary sister will be great. I've got everything all ready to welcome her to the family. I made up the guest room with my favorite sheets and put fresh towels in the guest bathroom. There's no desk in the guest room, so I cleared off some space on mine so she can use it to do her homework."

"Sounds like you thought of everything," Stevie remarked.

Carole laughed again. "I think I did," she admitted. "I even put a new bulb in the lamp on her bedside table. And Dad and I have been talking over ideas for a birthday gift for Marie. We want to get her something really special."

"Being your temporary sister sounds like a pretty good deal," Lisa said. She licked the last bit of marshmallow topping off her spoon and then leaned back in her seat. "I have an idea. Why don't Stevie and I meet you and Marie at Pine Hollow tomorrow after she arrives?"

"I don't think so," Carole said slowly. The idea was tempting, but she wasn't sure Marie would want to rush off to Pine Hollow as soon as she arrived. "It will be her first night at our house, and she'll probably need some time to get settled. And I'll have to be there to show her the ropes —kind of like you've been doing for Priscilla," she added to Stevie.

"Oh, all right," Lisa said. "How about the day after tomorrow? The four of us could go for a trail ride or something after school."

Carole shrugged. "Maybe," she said. She didn't want to

commit herself until she knew what Marie wanted to do. She was planning to be the perfect host so that Marie wouldn't have time to get homesick or miss her mother. Marie liked riding, but Carole knew that she also liked other things, like listening to music and watching movies. Carole didn't want to force her to spend more time at Pine Hollow than she wanted to—even if that meant Carole would have to give up some of her usual riding time. Marie certainly deserved a little happiness in her life right about now, and Carole was going to make sure she got it.

I'll be just like a sister to her, Carole promised herself with a smile.

4

THE NEXT DAY Carole arrived home from school just in time to meet Marie and Mrs. Dana.

"Hello, Olivia," Carole's father exclaimed, hurrying out to the car as Mrs. Dana got out. "You two are right on time." He gave her a hug.

"Hello, Mitch," Mrs. Dana replied. "If there's one thing I've learned after spending so much time with a Marine, it's the importance of punctuality."

"Aha!" Colonel Hanson said. "I'm glad to see that my good qualities are rubbing off on you."

Marie climbed out of the passenger seat. "Don't get too excited," she told Colonel Hanson. "Mom's just being careful because the last time she went on one of these trips, she almost missed her plane."

41

"Hush, child," Mrs. Dana said with a slightly embarrassed smile. She turned to Colonel Hanson. "Whatever happened to the good old days when children were seen and not heard?"

Colonel Hanson laughed heartily. "I don't think we ever had any of those particular good old days around here," he said, ruffling Carole's curly black hair.

"Neither did we, come to think of it," Mrs. Dana said with a sidelong glance at Marie, who grinned back innocently. "Come on, kiddo, help me with the bags." She opened the car's trunk and started to lift out a large suitcase.

"Please, ladies. Allow me," Colonel Hanson said gallantly. He grabbed Marie's two suitcases and led the way into the house. "Right this way. Could you get the door, Carole?"

Once inside, all four of them headed up to the guest bedroom, which was right across the hall from Carole's room. "You'll be staying in here, Marie," Carole said, opening the door and ushering Marie in ahead of her.

"Nice," Marie said, looking around.

Carole surveyed the room as well, satisfied with her efforts to make it cozy. The flowered spread was tucked in over fluffy pillows, and Carole had brought in a bright hooked rug from her own room to cover the wood floor beside the bed. A vase of sunflowers from Colonel Hanson's small garden added a splash of color to the dresser.

And to add the finishing touch, Carole's black cat, Snowball, was curled up on the bed.

"The room looks lovely, doesn't it, honey?" Mrs. Dana said, putting an arm around Marie's shoulders.

"It certainly does," Colonel Hanson said. "And I'll be the first to admit that I didn't have a thing to do with it. Carole fixed it up for you all by herself."

"She did a great job," Marie said.

Carole smiled at the compliment.

"But I'm a little surprised," Marie added. She stepped farther into the room and looked around, a puzzled look on her face.

"What do you mean, hon?" asked Mrs. Dana.

Marie shrugged. "Well, knowing that Carole did the decorating, I would expect to see some more horsey stuff. You know—some hay, maybe a saddle or two. Or at least a few dozen horse posters."

The adults laughed, but Carole blushed, thinking of the walls in her own room, every inch of which were covered with pictures and posters of horses. And once again she found herself wishing that Marie didn't have to be so sarcastic all the time.

"Are you hungry, Marie?" Carole asked, trying to change the subject. "We could go downstairs and fix ourselves a snack."

"Sounds good to me," Marie said.

"I'm one step ahead of you," Colonel Hanson said, set-ting Marie's suitcases down beside the dresser and then heading back out to the hallway. "Follow me."

He led the girls and Mrs. Dana downstairs to the kitchen. With a flourish he brought out a platter of chocolate-chip cookies from the oven.

"I've been keeping them warm for you," he said. "I baked them this afternoon from my own secret recipe." He winked at Carole.

"Yum!" Carole exclaimed. "You haven't made your secret-recipe cookies for ages, Dad!" She stopped to think. "In fact, I can't remember the last time you made them."

"Well, this is a special occasion," Colonel Hanson said. He pulled out a chair for Mrs. Dana, then quickly poured four glasses of cold milk. Soon all four of them were seated around the kitchen table, munching happily on the warm, delicious cookies.

"Now this is what I call an after-school snack," Marie said appreciatively, licking some melted chocolate off her fingers.

"Actually, I think this qualifies as an after-Marine-Corps snack," Carole joked.

Everyone laughed. "I guess that means it's also a preflight snack," Colonel Hanson said to Mrs. Dana. Then he smiled at Marie. "And a welcome-to-our-home snack, too."

Carole took another cookie and dunked it in her milk. She was proud of her father for making Marie feel so wel-

44

come. Colonel Hanson had always gotten along well with all of Carole's friends. It was just one of the many things she appreciated about having him as a father.

A few minutes later Mrs. Dana glanced at her watch. "Oh, my!" she said, jumping to her feet. "I'd better get a move on if I don't want to miss my plane."

Colonel Hanson got up, too. "We'll all walk you to the car."

Outside, Mrs. Dana turned to Marie. "Good-bye, darling," she said, grabbing Marie and giving her a tight hug. "Be good while I'm gone."

"I will," Marie said, her voice a little muffled by her mother's jacket. She pulled back. "Have fun in Europe."

Mrs. Dana hugged her again. "I'll try. And I hope you have a nice time here with Mitch and Carole. Have fun on your birthday, but save some celebrating to do when I get back."

"Thanks, Mom."

Finally Mrs. Dana let go of Marie long enough to give Colonel Hanson a big hug and a quick kiss. "Thanks so much for taking care of my baby for me, Mitch," she said.

"It will be a pleasure," he assured her. "Don't worry about a thing. Carole and I have it all under control."

Mrs. Dana gave Carole a hug, too. "Many thanks to you too, Carole," she said. "It's nice to know Marie will be staying with a friend."

"You're welcome," Carole replied. "Have a nice trip."

Finally Mrs. Dana gave Marie one last big hug and then got into the car. Carole, her father, and Marie waved and shouted good-byes as the car pulled out of the driveway and moved off down the road.

When it was out of sight, Carole turned to Marie. "Come on," she said. "I'll help you unpack."

"Good idea," Colonel Hanson said. "Meanwhile, I'll start dinner. Marie, I hope you like chicken and rice."

"Sure," Marie replied. "I'll eat almost anything that doesn't eat me first."

As Carole and Marie went upstairs and started to arrange Marie's things in the guest dresser, aided by the now wide-awake Snowball, Carole couldn't help thinking once again how much Marie had changed since she'd known her. The sullen, morose girl she'd first encountered at the hospital was gone. Marie was still direct and honest in her manner, as she had been then. But now she laughed more than she frowned, and she was friendlier and more talkative. Carole knew that all those changes meant that Marie had started to recover from her father's death and move on with her own life. It was the same process Carole herself had experienced after her mother had died. The fact that they'd both survived such a traumatic loss made Carole feel closer to Marie than anything else—it almost made them seem like *real* sisters.

Carole glanced over at Marie, wondering if she should share her thoughts. But Marie was looking annoyed. "I can't believe this," she said irritably, peering into one almost-empty suitcase and then the other.

"What's wrong?" Carole asked.

"I forgot my portable CD player," Marie said, checking the larger suitcase once more. Then she sat back with an irritated sigh. "How am I going to make it through two weeks without any music? I can't fall asleep without it!"

Carole smiled. "No problem," she reassured her. "You can use my clock radio while you're here. I have another alarm clock I can use."

"Really?" Marie exclaimed gratefully. "Thanks a lot, Carole. Hey, it doesn't just play the farm report or anything, does it?"

"Ha-ha," Carole replied, rolling her eyes. "No, it's a regular AM-FM radio. Come on, let's go get it." She hurried across the hall to her own room with Marie right behind her.

As soon as Marie stepped through the doorway, her eyes widened. "Hey, I guess I was right about your decorating taste," she commented, taking in the horse pictures and posters all around her. She wandered over to the window. "Oh, wow! You even have a poster taped to the window shade! That's wild!"

Carole decided to take that as a compliment, even if she wasn't quite convinced that Marie had meant it that way. "Here's the radio," she said, unplugging it and tucking it under her arm. "Come on, let's go set it up in your room."

She smiled with pleasure at her own words, forgetting about Marie's comment. It was nice to think of the guest room as Marie's bedroom.

A few minutes later the radio was in place on the bedside table in Marie's room. Marie switched it on and flipped around between channels until she found a song she liked. "Hey, this is one of my favorites," she exclaimed happily. She started humming along as she and Carole returned to unpacking. Carole hummed along, too, even though she'd heard the song only a few times. She decided that if she could just get used to Marie's jokes, the visit was sure to be practically perfect.

MARIE LEANED BACK in her chair. "I'm so full I may never eat again," she declared. "That was a wonderful dinner, Colonel."

"I'm glad you liked it," he replied, beaming at her. "The chicken is my own special recipe."

"You sure do have a lot of special recipes," Marie teased him.

"Aha, a joker," Colonel Hanson said. "I can see we're going to have a good time while you're here, Marie." He smiled. "I'm glad you're staying here while your mother is gone. It will be a lot of fun to have two girls in the house."

Carole smiled and agreed. She was having fun so far. Before dinner she and Marie had listened to music for a while. Then Stevie had called to say hello to Marie. That had given Carole a chance to talk to her father about what to get Marie for her birthday. They'd come up with a few good ideas before Stevie and Marie had finished their conversation. Then, a few minutes later, Lisa had called. While Marie talked to her, Carole and her father made plans to go shopping together later in the week. Carole promised to ask Stevie and Lisa to take Marie off their hands and keep her distracted so she wouldn't suspect what they were doing.

After they had helped Colonel Hanson clear the table, Carole and Marie headed upstairs to start their homework. "You can have the desk to yourself tonight," Carole told Marie, shuffling through her backpack. "I have to write a two-page essay for English class, so I'll be downstairs using Dad's computer." She pulled out her English notebook and her dog-eared copy of *Of Mice and Men* and headed down to the living room.

Carole was still on the first paragraph of her essay when Marie came into the room.

"Uh, hi, Carole," Marie said. "When you said you had a paper to write, that reminded me that I'm supposed to write one, too. It's for extra credit in my social-studies class. Do you think I could use the computer when you're finished?"

Carole bit her lip. She knew she should offer to let Marie do her work first, since she was a guest. On the other hand, Marie's paper was only for extra credit, while

49

Carole's was an assignment. She hesitated for a moment, not sure what to say.

Colonel Hanson had entered the room just in time to hear Marie's question. "Carole, why don't you let Marie do her assignment first? She's our guest, you know." His tone was faintly reproving. Carole immediately felt guilty.

"I was just going to say the same thing," she said quickly. She saved her document and then got up from the chair. "Go ahead, Marie. I can finish later."

"Are you sure?" Marie said, sitting down. "Thanks a lot, Carole."

Colonel Hanson smiled at the two girls. "Actually, Carole, I was just coming out here to rustle up a volunteer to help me with the dishes," he said. "How about it?"

"Sure, Dad," Carole said. She followed him out to the kitchen. "I'll wash and you can dry."

They got to work. As Carole plunged her hands into the warm, soapy water, she realized that for once she was glad to be doing the dishes. She liked having Marie around, but after spending the whole afternoon as a threesome, it was nice to have a few minutes alone with her father.

"You know, Carole," Colonel Hanson said, interrupting her thoughts, "I've been wanting to talk to you alone ever since Marie got here."

"What is it, Dad?" Carole asked, handing him a freshly washed bowl.

"It's about Marie," he said seriously. "I just wanted to

50

make sure you know how important it is that we give her extra-special care. It hasn't been that long since she lost her father, and it's sure to be tough on her to have her mother so far away for such a long time."

"I understand," Carole said. "I'm being nice to Marie. And I've got a lot of special things planned for her, especially on her birthday."

"That's good, honey," Colonel Hanson said. "But it's important to remember to be nice and consider Marie's feelings in little ways as well as big ones. For instance, I noticed you took the last of the rice at dinner without asking Marie if she wanted more."

Carole frowned. "I guess so, but she already had lots of rice on her plate."

"Even so, you should have asked," Colonel Hanson said.

Carole didn't really think it was fair for her father to criticize her for something so ridiculous, but she reminded herself that he was just anxious to keep Marie happy. Carole was, too. "Don't worry," she told her father with a smile. "The rice incident was a fluke. I'm going to be *very* nice to Marie while she's staying with us, I promise. In fact, I was thinking of taking her riding tomorrow after school. What could be nicer than that?"

Colonel Hanson laughed. "Not much, in your book," he admitted. Seemingly satisfied by Carole's response, he changed the subject, and they finished the rest of the dishes quickly, working as a team.

"STEVIE, I ABSOLUTELY love your belt," Priscilla exclaimed as she set her tray down across the lunchroom table from Stevie's. "I've been meaning to tell you all day."

"Thanks," Stevie said. The belt was a nice leather one that had been a gift from her parents for her last birthday. "I like your whole outfit."

"Do you really?" Priscilla asked, looking pleased. "I'm so glad! I wasn't sure it was working for me." As usual Priscilla was impeccably dressed in a perfectly coordinated outfit. Her shoes matched her belt, which matched her small handbag. Her shirt and pants were spotlessly clean and wrinkle free.

"You always look great, Priscilla," Stevie told her. She wrinkled her nose at the food on the trays in front of them.

"Unfortunately the Fenton Hall mystery meat isn't so lucky."

Priscilla laughed. "You have the best sense of humor, Stevie," she said admiringly. "No wonder you're so popular."

"I wish Ms. Lebrun agreed with you," Stevie said.

"She's your French teacher, right?" Priscilla said. "See, I'm learning! Before long I'll know Fenton Hall as well as you do."

"You're a fast learner," Stevie agreed, taking a tentative bite of the meat on her tray.

"It's only because you're such a good teacher," Priscilla replied. "So what's Lebrun's problem with your sense of humor?"

"Well, to make a long story short, *someone* replaced her French tape with a Spanish one," Stevie said with a grin. "For some reason she seems to think that someone was me. Can you imagine?"

Just then Patty Featherstone walked by. *"Buenos días,* Stevie," she said with a laugh.

"Hi, Patty," Stevie said. "I was just telling Priscilla about what happened in our French class. You know Priscilla, don't you?"

"Yes, we've met," Patty said, glancing briefly at Priscilla. "Anyway, Stevie, I just wanted to congratulate you. Your prank was a riot!"

"It was nothing," Stevie replied modestly. "Hey, would

53

you like to join us? Maybe I can come up with another brilliant prank involving this mystery meat."

"Maybe some other time," Patty said. "I promised Christina I'd sit with her today. *Adiós!*" She waved and walked off, chuckling.

"I'm just lucky Ms. Lebrun gave me an extra homework assignment instead of detention," Stevie said, turning back to Priscilla. "Carole and Lisa would kill me if I had to stay late today. I'm supposed to meet them at Pine Hollow right after school. Today's the day I'm supposed to ask Max about using the hayloft for Saturday's sleepover."

"Really?" Priscilla said. "Well, if you need any help with your assignment, just let me know. I'm pretty good in French."

"Thanks," Stevie said, a little distractedly. She was still thinking about her plans for that afternoon. "Carole's friend Marie—she's the one whose birthday is coming up, you know—is coming to Pine Hollow today, too. She's a pretty good rider, but she hasn't been on a horse in a while. We're taking her on a trail ride." She was still hoping to interest Priscilla in riding.

"That's nice," Priscilla said. "Hey, did I mention what Mr. Rose said about my latest drawings for his class?"

"What?" Stevie asked, disappointed that Priscilla still didn't seem interested in anything she said about Pine Hollow.

"He said they were really original," Priscilla said. "He

said he hadn't had a student who could draw as well as me for at least five years."

"That's great, Priscilla. Maybe you can be an artist when you grow up," Stevie said.

"Actually, I'd like to be a fashion designer," Priscilla said. "I already told you that, remember? I've got lots of ideas already. Maybe I'll even move to Paris. Wouldn't that be incredible?"

"Sounds like fun," Stevie agreed. "Speaking of fun, you should come with me to Pine Hollow sometime. Not today, since Marie will be there already and we'll have to help her, but sometime soon. You'll never believe how great riding is until you try it."

"Honestly, Stevie," Priscilla said with a laugh. "You and your friends Lisa and Carole have one-track minds."

"Oh, I almost forgot to ask, how did you like meeting them?" Stevie asked eagerly.

"They seemed sort of nice," Priscilla said slowly. "Although they were a little obsessive about horses. I mean, there is more to life, you know. I guess those two just haven't figured it out yet. Especially the one who thinks she's the real expert—was that Lisa or Carole?"

"Carole," Stevie said. She wasn't particularly good at hiding her feelings, so she had to make an extra effort not to show Priscilla how annoyed she was at her remarks about her friends. She's new, Stevie reminded herself, gritting her teeth. She just doesn't know them very well. *And* she doesn't know how interesting horses and riding can be.

"Anyway," Priscilla said, "I just don't think I have much in common with them. I can usually tell right away whether I like someone. For instance, I knew as soon as I met you that I liked you."

"Hmm," Stevie said noncommittally. She decided to change the subject to something Priscilla might be more interested in: shopping. "After our trail ride Lisa and I are going shopping for a birthday present for Marie. Carole's going to help her father pick out something for the two of them, so Lisa and I are on our own. We want to find something really great."

"That's nice," Priscilla said. Stevie was beginning to think that was her favorite phrase. "But actually, I was just going to ask if you'd be able to do your trail ride and stuff another time. I was hoping we could get together after school today. Maybe we could go to your house so I could look at those old Fenton Hall yearbooks you were telling me about last week. I think that would really give me a feel for the history of this place and help me feel at home here."

"Sorry," Stevie said. "I just can't do it today. My friends are counting on me to talk to Max. And I told you, it's Marie's first ride in a while—I want to be there for that. *And* I don't know when Lisa and I will get another chance to go shopping."

"Okay, okay," Priscilla said, holding up her hands. "I was just asking."

The bell rang. Lunch period was over. "I'd better get going," Stevie said, standing and picking up her tray. "My math teacher doesn't like us to be late, and I don't want to get any other teachers mad at me today."

"Okay," said Priscilla. "I'll see you in biology. Save me a seat."

Stevie nodded. But she couldn't help thinking that her friendship with Priscilla wasn't going quite the way she had imagined it.

THERE WERE FIVE minutes left in Carole's English class when a student she didn't recognize came into the room and handed a folded piece of paper to the teacher.

Ms. Blackburn read the note. "Carole, could you come up here, please?" she said.

Surprised, Carole went up to the teacher's desk. "What is it?"

"Your father is on the phone for you," Ms. Blackburn said. "You're excused to go to the principal's office to take the call."

Carole followed the messenger out of the room and down the hall toward the principal's office, her head spinning. Why would her father be calling her at school? The last time he'd done that had been when Carole was eleven. He'd been calling then to tell her that they were taking her mother to the hospital again, and that he would be coming to pick up Carole shortly. Mrs. Hanson had died a few days later.

Carole gulped. She tried to put that terrible memory out of her head and think positively. If her father was calling her, nothing too bad could have happened to him. But what if something terrible had happened to someone else? A relative, Stevie or Lisa, Starlight . . . the possibilities were too frightening to think about.

By the time she reached the office and picked up the phone the secretary handed her, she was so nervous that she could barely squeak out the word, "Hello?"

"Carole? Is that you?" Colonel Hanson said, his voice as cheerful as always.

"It's me, Dad," Carole said. "What's wrong?"

"Listen, honey," her father said. "I just thought I'd better call to remind you about the juice. I know you were pretty sleepy this morning, and I was afraid you'd forget."

"The juice?" Carole repeated. She didn't have the foggiest idea what he was talking about. She *had* been sleepy that morning—in fact, she still was. Marie had kept the radio on until almost midnight the night before. It had been loud enough to keep Carole awake, but she hadn't wanted to ask Marie to turn it down. After all, she was a guest.

"That's what I was afraid of," Colonel Hanson said reproachfully. "Remember, I told you and Marie that we only had one insulated cooler bag, so I put both your juice boxes in it with your lunch. You'll need to give Marie her juice box at lunch. I know you two have different lunch periods, so I thought I'd better remind you."

"Thanks, Dad," Carole said mechanically. She did remember the conversation now, and in fact she *had* forgotten all about having Marie's juice. Still, she couldn't quite believe that was why her father had had her dragged out of class. "Are you sure that's all?"

"That's it, sweetie," he said. "Now, don't forget, okay?"

"I won't. I promise," she said. " 'Bye."

She hung up the phone. The school secretary stopped typing and looked up. "Everything all right, hon?" she asked. "I hope there's nothing wrong at home."

"No, no, everything's fine," Carole assured her. "It's under control." She left the office, still feeling a little confused. When her head began to clear, her confusion turned to relief, then annoyance, then anger. The relief was because there really was no emergency. The annoyance was with her father for frightening her. And the anger was for Marie.

Having Marie as a guest should have been fun. And in some ways, Carole had to admit, it was fun. But it was also turning out to be more difficult than Carole had expected. Last night her father had gotten carried away about Marie's having enough rice, and today he'd dragged Carole out of class just to make sure Marie had her juice. When was the last time the Colonel had been that worried about what *Carole* had for lunch? He certainly hadn't seemed concerned last night when Carole had had to stay up late finishing her English essay after Marie stopped working on the computer. And did he even know that when the essay was finally finished, Carole hadn't been able to sleep because Marie was playing the radio too loud?

In fact, the more Carole thought about it, the more she realized that Marie's visit was totally upsetting the Hansons' life—and she hadn't even been there twenty-four hours yet! Carole even found herself missing her father's fifties and sixties music. She hadn't heard anything but current rock hits since Marie had come to stay.

By this time the late bell had rung and students were hurrying to get to first lunch period. That was when Marie ate lunch. There was no way Carole would be able to make it to her next class on time, especially since she still had to find Marie and give her the juice box. That would be just one more thing for someone to chew her out for, she thought peevishly. Feeling very sorry for herself, she headed toward her locker to get Marie's juice.

ACROSS TOWN AT Fenton Hall, Stevie was sitting in math class pretending to pay attention to the long, complicated problem that Bobby Effingwell was solving at the board. But actually she was thinking about Priscilla. Stevie didn't have anything against art or fashion, but they weren't topics she enjoyed discussing very often. And she had a sneaking suspicion that Priscilla felt the same way about horses.

It was finally dawning on Stevie that she and Priscilla just didn't have much in common aside from attending the same school. And the worst part was that Priscilla didn't like Stevie's two best friends in the world. As much as she would have liked a new friend at Fenton Hall, Stevie realized that Priscilla might not be the person for the job.

When math class finally ended, Stevie hurried to biology class. She saved a seat for Priscilla, who arrived a moment later.

"Stevie, I just had a great idea," Priscilla said breathlessly as she sat down. "Since we can't get together today, why don't you come to my house for a sleepover on Saturday night? You could bring those yearbooks, and we could rent some movies or something."

Stevie stared at her. "Priscilla, you know I have that sleepover with my friends on Saturday," she said. "I mean, come on, it's all I've been talking about for days!"

Priscilla shrugged. "Well, I know, but you don't really have to do that, do you?" she said. "I thought you'd be excited to have another offer. I mean, who really wants to sleep in a stinky old barn anyway?"

"That's it," Stevie exclaimed. Now she knew for sure that she was right about Priscilla. She took a deep breath, trying to think of the best way to say what she had to say. "Priscilla, this isn't working out."

"What isn't?"

"Our being friends and hanging out together," Stevie said. "I'm sorry. It's not that you're not a nice person. I just don't think we have much in common. I mean, I like horses, you like clothes, I like my riding friends, you don't —I just don't think it's going to work. I'm really sorry."

Stevie was afraid Priscilla would be hurt, even though she'd tried to be as tactful as possible. But instead the other girl just shrugged. "Well, all right, if that's the way you feel," she said. "Thanks for showing me around." Without another word Priscilla turned to the student sitting behind her, Coreen Maloney. "Hi there, I'm Priscilla Tyler. Aren't we in the same art class? It's Coreen, right?"

As she listened to Priscilla chatting with Coreen, Stevie shook her head in disbelief. People were certainly full of surprises. She would have thought Priscilla would be crushed to hear that her new best friend didn't want to hang out with her anymore—especially after she'd been telling Stevie all week how much she liked her. But from the sound of things, Coreen had already been auditioned and accepted as Stevie's replacement.

It's just as well, Stevie decided as the teacher called the class to order. Now she could really concentrate on Marie and the sleepover. To begin with, she vowed to spend this class period figuring out the best way to ask Max for his permission to use the hayloft.

6

"Bingo!" Stevie cried triumphantly as she emerged from Max's office that afternoon.

"He okayed it?" Marie asked.

"He sure did," Stevie replied, throwing an arm around Marie's shoulders and grinning at her.

"Was it hard to convince him?" Lisa asked.

"Not at all, thanks to my superb negotiating skills," Stevie said. "Well, actually, that was only part of it. He was in a good mood because he and Deborah have finally ze-roed in on the perfect china pattern. *And* he said he'd been looking for something special to do for our guest of honor while her mom is away." She winked at Marie.

"I guess that makes it just about unanimous, then, doesn't it?" Carole muttered. She'd been stewing all afternoon long about the juice-box incident, and she wasn't feeling particularly friendly toward Marie right then.

Stevie turned to stare at Carole in surprise, her arm dropping from Marie's shoulder. Carole's comment had sounded almost nasty. Stevie caught Lisa's eye and shrugged. Lisa shrugged back. Neither of them knew what was bugging their friend, but they figured they'd find out sooner or later.

"Come on, let's hit the trail," Lisa said. "I'll help you find Chip's tack if you want, Marie." Max had suggested that Marie ride Chippewa, an even-tempered Appaloosa gelding, on the trail ride that day.

"Thanks," Marie said gratefully. "I can never find what I'm looking for in that tack room. It's a worse mess than my bedroom."

Lisa and Stevie laughed, but Carole frowned, annoyed at Marie's criticism. It was true that the Pine Hollow tack room *looked* like a disaster area, with bridles, saddles, and other equipment covering every square inch of space. But in reality it was all very organized, with a specific place for everything. You just had to learn the system. Carole opened her mouth to tell Marie so, but then she noticed the grin on the other girl's face and realized she had been joking. Carole watched Marie and Lisa walk off toward the tack room, chattering and laughing together like old friends, and bit her lip. Was she really the only one who found Marie's sense of humor irritating? She shook her head and headed for Starlight's stall.

A few minutes later all four girls' horses were tacked up and ready to go. The girls mounted, brushed the good-luck horseshoe on the wall, and set off at a leisurely walk. Stevie was riding first on Topside, with Lisa behind her on Prancer, then Marie on Chip. Carole and Starlight brought up the rear.

"Don't forget, you guys, I'm a little rusty," Marie commented as they crossed a field toward the woods. "I don't spend every waking moment on horseback like you do, so I might need a refresher lesson."

"Don't worry, I'll help you," Carole said. "From back here I'll be able to see what you're doing wrong. For instance, right now your heels should be down more, and your arms look a little stiff."

Marie obediently adjusted her position. "Better?"

"A little, but now you're leaning back too much, and your legs are too far forward. You look like you're sitting in a chair."

"Oops," Marie said quietly. Again she adjusted her position in the saddle.

"Okay, that's a little better," Carole said crisply. "Now let's work on the way you're holding the reins. Don't curl your wrists, and keep your thumbs pointing up and your elbows in. And stop twisting around to look at me! You're going to confuse your horse. You've got to keep your eyes looking in the direction you want to go."

Stevie broke that particular rule for a second by twisting around to catch a glimpse of Marie's face. Marie looked harried, and no wonder. Carole barely seemed to pause for breath as she continued to bark out instructions. Lisa looked as surprised as Stevie felt at Carole's behavior. Carole never hesitated to give advice to anyone who asked for it and a lot of people who didn't. But usually that advice was helpful and constructive. The advice she was giving Marie sounded more like plain old criticism, and that wasn't like Carole at all.

A few minutes later the girls heard the sound of hoofbeats on the trail ahead of them. Carole paused in her barrage of advice as the four of them saw Simon Atherton riding toward them on Patch. Simon wasn't Stevie's favorite person at Pine Hollow, but at this moment she was glad to see him. She would have welcomed any interruption to Carole's drill-sergeant routine.

"Hi, Simon," she said. "What are you doing out here all by yourself?" One of Max's strictest rules was that nobody was allowed to ride out on the trails alone. It was important always to have at least one other person nearby just in case something went wrong.

"Oh, gosh, hi, Stephanie," Simon said, bringing Patch to a stop with some difficulty. "Hi, everyone. I didn't start out alone. Veronica was riding Garnet out, so I offered to go with her so she could go on the trails. But I think she forgot that I'm kind of new at riding, and she cantered so far ahead that I kind of lost her. I was just heading back. I hope she's all right."

"I'm sure she's fine," Lisa said dryly. Veronica diAngelo was a spoiled rich girl who boarded her purebred Arabian mare at Pine Hollow. It didn't surprise any of them that Veronica had planned to ride Garnet out alone despite Max's rules. Veronica seemed to think that most rules were made for other people to follow and for her to break.

It surprised The Saddle Club even less that Veronica had apparently gone out of her way to lose Simon. Ever since Stevie had schemed to get Veronica and Simon to go out on a date, he had been following Veronica around like a lovesick puppy. No matter how mean she was to him, he never got the hint, and so he ended up driving her crazy. Stevie considered that something of a personal triumph. But she didn't bother to gloat over that at the moment, because she knew that most of the trail they were on wasn't safe at a canter. She also knew that Veronica would never bother to think about that, especially when she was trying to get away from Simon. Stevie just hoped that Garnet hadn't injured herself.

"So who's your new buddy?" Simon asked, looking at Marie.

Stevie quickly introduced them. "Marie is staying with

Carole for two weeks. To celebrate, this is her first trail ride."

"Are you an experienced rider?" Simon asked Marie.

"Well, I used to be an intermediate one, but I'm a little out of practice," Marie explained.

"Yes," Lisa said. "Carole has been giving her some—er—pointers."

"Gosh, that's great," Simon said. "Carole really knows her stuff. Well, I'd better get going."

Marie glanced at Carole, then at Simon. "If you don't mind, I'd like to ride back with you," she said. "I'm kind of tired. And I think these guys might have more fun without me—I think I'm even rustier than I realized."

"Sure, no problem," said Simon cheerfully. "Let's hit the old trail."

"You don't mind, do you, Carole?" Marie asked as she turned Chip out of the line.

Carole shrugged. "It's fine with me. You don't want to wear yourself out."

"Right," said Marie. "And this way I'll be there to meet your father. He should be coming to pick us up pretty soon." She urged Chip forward after Patch, who had started ambling off toward home without bothering to wait for a signal from Simon. "I'll see you all in a while."

As Simon and Marie disappeared from sight, Stevie remarked, "It's unusual for your father to pick you up on a weekday, isn't it, Carole?"

"Yeah, well, a lot of unusual things have been going on around here lately," Carole snapped.

Lisa and Stevie traded glances. They had a feeling that a change of subject would do them all good.

"So, Stevie, did you ever convince your new friend Priscilla to try riding?" Lisa asked.

Stevie touched Topside lightly with her heel, and he obediently moved off down the trail. "Not exactly," Stevie replied. "In fact, I've been meaning to tell you guys what happened." She quickly related her conversations with Priscilla at lunch and in biology class. "I finally realized that she wanted me as a friend, all right—but only if she could have me all to herself. She didn't even care that she was asking me to give up all kinds of things that are really important to me, like you guys, for instance. As soon as I realized that, I had to call it quits with her. Nothing is going to split up The Saddle Club, and that's that."

"And that's just what you told her?" Lisa asked.

Stevie nodded. "More or less. She took it better than I expected and went in search of a new best friend. Problem solved."

"I just wish my problem were that simple," Carole said, biting her lip.

"What do you mean?" Lisa and Stevie asked in a single voice.

Carole just shrugged in reply.

Before her friends could press her further, they were distracted by Prancer. The high-strung Thoroughbred seemed suddenly to have decided she didn't want to be on a trail ride after all. Without warning she skittered to one side, almost banging into a tree. A surprised Lisa barely managed to keep her seat. Prancer shook her head and pawed at the ground. Lisa was riding between Stevie and Carole for a reason, though—not only was she the least experienced rider of the three, but Prancer was the least experienced trail horse. Now, with Topside ahead of her on the narrow trail and Starlight behind, the skittish mare had no place to go. She came to a dead halt and snorted.

"Quick, tighten up on the reins before she tries anything else," Carole said. "You want to make sure she knows you're in charge and paying attention."

Lisa nodded ruefully as she did as Carole said. "Apparently she could tell that I wasn't paying much attention to her a second ago," she admitted.

"Don't worry about it too much," Carole advised. "It happens to everybody once in a while. Just be extra careful for the rest of the ride so it doesn't stick in her mind that she got away with anything."

"I will," Lisa said. "Thanks."

They decided to head back to the stable. On the way Lisa concentrated on keeping her horse under control and making sure she knew who was in charge. Prancer behaved so beautifully most of the time that it was easy to forget that all this was still fairly new to her. Lisa really hadn't been paying close enough attention back there, and that wasn't good. She knew that a horse was only as good as its rider, and so she vowed to try to do better from now on.

Stevie was concerned about Prancer, too, but she was even more concerned about someone else. She had a feeling she had just figured out what was bugging Carole, and she vowed to keep a close eye on her to see if she was right.

Carole was keeping a watchful eye on Prancer in case of further problems, but she was also thinking. She realized, belatedly, that she had been pretty mean to Marie on the trail—in fact, it was almost as though she hadn't been able to stop herself. She'd been as out of control as Prancer, but though the horse's misbehavior was easy to understand, Carole's wasn't. Even if Marie had been sort of annoying since she'd arrived the day before, and even if Colonel Hanson had been acting strangely because of her visit, it wasn't very polite to take it out on Marie. After all, Marie was a guest in their home. And Carole had to remember that everyone was different. Just because Marie had a weird sense of humor and was obsessed with rock music, it didn't mean Carole didn't like her. It just meant she'd have to adjust to living with her.

I'm overtired, Carole finally decided, that's all—and still a little shaky from the scare Dad's phone call gave me this morning. As The Saddle Club turned their horses into the paddock at Pine Hollow, Carole reminded herself that Marie was missing her mother and needed an understanding friend—no, make that *sister*. Carole vowed once again to be that sister to her if she could.

WHEN THE SADDLE CLUB reached the stable a few minutes later, the first person they saw was Marie. She was leaning against a fence post near the driveway, humming and kicking at the dirt with the toe of one of Carole's old riding boots, which she had borrowed.

"Hi, guys," she greeted them, coming to meet them as they dismounted and started to lead the horses inside. "The Colonel isn't here yet, so I can give you a hand with the horses if you want."

"Not necessary, Marie," Carole answered before Stevie or Lisa could say a word. She was determined to keep her vow, and she was starting now. "You can just wait here. Everything's under control." Carole turned and led Starlight into the stable, proud of herself for realizing that

Marie shouldn't be stuck doing extra stable chores. After all, she was a guest.

Stevie and Lisa glanced at each other as Carole disappeared inside. Now Carole didn't seem to want Marie around at all. They shrugged, then turned back to Marie.

"We'll see you in a few minutes," Lisa told Marie.

Marie nodded. "Okay," she said quietly. Lisa thought she looked a little hurt.

"Hey, Carole," Lisa said when they were out of Marie's earshot, "maybe we should let Marie help us. There's no better way for her to learn about horses than by helping out with superfun stuff like grooming and mucking out stalls."

"Not necessary," Carole said again, apparently not noticing Lisa's attempt at humor. "She's a guest. She shouldn't have to do any work."

"Well, yeah," Lisa said slowly, "but I think she may be feeling a little left out. She may think you don't want her around or something."

"Lisa's right," Stevie added. "I think Marie really wanted to help out."

Carole frowned. She couldn't believe her two best friends were criticizing her just when she was trying her hardest to be extra nice to Marie. It was as if everyone except Carole had been taken over by aliens. First her father was turning into a different person around Marie, and now Lisa and Stevie were, too. "Give me a break,"

74

Carole said sharply. "Marie doesn't have to hang out with us every single second, you know."

Lisa was more than a little surprised at Carole's attitude. "Stevie," she whispered when she was sure Carole wouldn't hear, "what's up with her?"

Stevie glanced at Carole. "Mini–Saddle Club meeting, you and me," she whispered back. "As soon as Carole and Marie leave."

Lisa nodded and turned off as they reached Prancer's stall. "I'll be there."

AFTER THE HORSES were untacked, groomed, and comfortably settled in their stalls, Carole, Stevie, and Lisa joined Marie outside.

"We'll keep you company while you wait," Lisa offered.

"Great," Marie said. Carole didn't say anything. She just crossed her arms across her chest and stared straight ahead, her face frozen in a frown.

"So, Marie," Stevie said, trying to make casual conversation. "What's that song you were humming just now?"

"It's called 'Let Me Be Me,'" Marie told her. She hummed a little bit more. "It's by the Three Blind Mice. They're my favorite band."

"Oh, yeah, I think I know them," Lisa said. "They do that song 'Lori Lori Lori,' right?"

Stevie nodded and started whistling the song Lisa had

mentioned. "I love that song. My brother Alex has the tape."

Marie smiled. "I have a lot of their CDs at home, and they're really great. I'll play them for you sometime if you want. It'll have to be after my mom gets back, though, because I forgot to bring them to Carole's house."

"Yeah, we know, we've heard all about it," Carole muttered darkly.

Stevie and Lisa noticed that Marie pretended not to hear the comment, but they knew that she had. And they knew that it bothered her, because she didn't say another word the whole time they were waiting.

Luckily they didn't have very long to wait. The Hansons' familiar blue station wagon pulled into the drive a moment later. "Hello, girls!" Colonel Hanson greeted the four of them, climbing out of the car. "How was your ride?"

"Pretty good," Stevie said. "We had a little trouble with Prancer, though."

Colonel Hanson nodded wisely. He was a parent volunteer for Horse Wise, the Pine Hollow branch of the U.S. Pony Club, and so he knew all the horses at Pine Hollow. "I'm sure with The Saddle Club training her, that mare will be a wonderful stable horse in no time at all." He turned to Marie. "Did you have fun, Marie?"

"Sure," she said. "Riding a horse is sort of like riding a bike. You never really forget it once you've learned." She rubbed the backs of her thighs and grimaced. "Although my rear end always seems to forget everything *it* ever knew. I think I was posting down every time Chip was coming up."

Colonel Hanson laughed. "You're a funny girl, Marie."

"Yeah," Carole said flatly. "Hilarious."

Colonel Hanson didn't seem to notice her sarcasm. "Come on, you two, let's get going," he said. "I had a great idea for dinner tonight. Marie, since you were telling us yesterday how much you like pizza, I thought we could have a make-your-own-pie party, just the three of us. How does that sound?"

"It sounds terrific to me!" Stevie said hungrily.

Colonel Hanson laughed again and winked at Marie. "Sorry, Stevie, this one's just for family. Maybe next time we'll invite you."

"Aw, you mean you don't consider me part of the family?" Stevie said, pretending to be hurt.

"Not when it comes to food," Colonel Hanson joked.

"What are we waiting for?" Marie demanded, opening the passenger-side door and hopping in. "Let's get at those pizzas!"

"That's what I like—a girl with an appetite," Colonel Hanson said. He glanced at Carole. "Come on, honey, let's move out."

Carole shrugged and headed for the car. "I guess I'm sitting in the backseat again," she said quietly.

Neither Colonel Hanson nor Marie heard her. But

Stevie and Lisa did. "I think we'd better have that Saddle Club meeting," Lisa commented as the station wagon pulled out of the driveway.

Stevie nodded. "And fast!"

As Stevie and Lisa walked toward the shopping center a few minutes later, Lisa took a big breath of the fresh air. Even though the weather was still warm, she thought she could detect the slightest hint of autumn sharpness in it. "You know, I feel bad for saying this, but it's a relief to have Carole and Marie gone," she remarked. "Things were getting pretty tense back there."

"You're not kidding," Stevie said. "And I think I know why."

"Let's hear it."

Stevie sighed. "I think Carole is suffering from good old sibling rivalry."

"Sibling rivalry?" Lisa repeated. "But Marie's not Carole's real sister. She's just been calling her that."

"True. But Carole is jealous because Marie has been getting a lot of attention from her dad," Stevie explained. "So Carole has been taking it out on Marie, even though Marie herself hasn't really done anything wrong. That way Carole gets her father's attention, even if it's only to have him yell at her. It's sort of like the time my brother Michael dropped my dad's brand-new watch down the toilet."

"What?" Lisa looked confused.

"You see, it was the night of my other brother Chad's debut in his school play. Everyone was paying a lot of attention to Chad and none to Michael, even though Michael had just made the Pee Wee soccer team. He was mad, so he did something he knew would get everyone's attention. And there you have it: sibling rivalry."

"I think I see," Lisa said. "Carole's used to having her dad all to herself, so it's hard for her to share him. Even if it's only for two weeks."

"Exactly," said Stevie. "And believe me, with three pain-in-the-neck brothers like mine, I know what I'm talking about."

Lisa thought about it for a minute. "I guess I can sort of understand how she feels," she said finally. "My brother is so much older that I'm practically like an only child myself —after all, he doesn't live with us and we hardly ever see him." She shook her head. "I know I complain sometimes when my parents pay *too* much attention to me, but I don't know how well I'd handle it if they were suddenly paying lots of attention to somebody else."

Stevie nodded. She remembered that Lisa had first started riding at Pine Hollow because her mother had insisted on it. Mrs. Atwood had insisted that Lisa do lots of other things, too, from ballet lessons to tennis. But once Lisa had discovered how much she loved riding, *she* had finally insisted on giving up the other things she didn't like so much. Since then she and her mother had had a much better relationship, though Mrs. Atwood could still be overbearing at times.

"How do you deal with having all those brothers, Stevie?" Lisa asked.

"Well, my parents do most of the coping, I guess," Stevie admitted. "When we start fighting or something, they'll threaten to cut off our allowances or our TV or phone privileges. When they're really mad at me, they'll sometimes threaten to cut off Pine Hollow. That almost always works."

By this time the girls had reached the shopping center. They stopped and looked around at the stores.

"Where should we start looking for Marie's present?" Stevie wondered. "Maybe we should try The Saddlery. We've found some great gifts there."

Lisa shook her head. "I have a better idea," she said. "I get the impression that Marie really likes rock music. Let's buy her something at Sights 'n' Sounds."

"Good idea," Stevie agreed. "Between us we should have enough money to get her a CD."

As the girls flipped through racks of CDs, they returned to their conversation about Carole.

"We need to do something before her behavior really gets out of hand," Lisa said seriously. "I mean, Marie's only been around for one day, and Carole's already turned into a different person. We both know that she has the best of intentions about Marie. She really wants to make this visit a good one. But she's sabotaging herself."

"Definitely," Stevie said. She wouldn't have used a ten-cent word like "sabotaging," but she knew what Lisa meant. She pulled out a CD. "Hey, here's a brand-new disk by the Three Blind Mice. Isn't that the band Marie was just talking about?"

"It sure is," Lisa said. "And if this disk is new, she probably doesn't have it yet. It's perfect."

They took the CD to the counter to pay for it. "This one's on sale," the sales clerk told them as he rang it up. "Thirty percent off."

"Are you thinking what I'm thinking?" Stevie asked Lisa as the clerk handed them their change.

"Unless I'm sadly mistaken, you're thinking that the only way to spend this extra money is on a couple of sundaes at TD's," Lisa guessed.

Stevie grinned. "You know me too well," she said. "Anyway, I could use some ice cream right about now to help me think. Because I may be getting an idea about what we can do to help Carole and Marie."

8

"So what's your bright idea?" Lisa asked a few minutes later. She and Stevie were seated in a booth at TD's waiting for their ice cream to arrive.

"Wait," Stevie said mysteriously. "I told you, I need food for thought."

Luckily the place wasn't very crowded, and their sundaes arrived a moment later. As soon as Stevie had swallowed a few bites of caramel topping on strawberry ice cream, she was ready to talk.

"What I figure is, Carole is sick and tired of everybody being so nice to Marie," she told Lisa.

"We already know that," Lisa said with a shrug.

"Just listen. What we have to do is figure out some way to make Carole really want to be nice to Marie herself."

"Mmm-hmm," said Lisa, taking another bite of her hot-fudge sundae. "But how do we do that?"

"It's simple," Stevie stated matter-of-factly. "We have to get Carole to save Marie's life."

Lisa almost choked on her ice cream. "Excuse me?"

"You know, put her in some deadly peril," Stevie explained. "Don't you watch TV or go to the movies?"

"Yes," Lisa replied. "But—"

Stevie was too caught up in the scheme that was forming in her mind to hear Lisa out. "What if Marie was about to be trampled by a runaway horse and Carole was the only one who could save her?" she went on.

"Have you lost your mind?" Lisa asked in disbelief. "Do you want to help Marie, or kill her?"

"Well, maybe the horse thing would be a little too risky," Stevie admitted. "But if we could set it up so Carole *thinks* Marie is in danger, even if she isn't really, then she'd have to look past her own petty jealousy and save her life. And that would make her see how much she really cares about Marie, and then she'd be sure to forget about all that rivalry stuff for the rest of Marie's visit. It's just like the way I was when Alex was sick."

Stevie's twin brother, Alex, had recently had a serious case of meningitis. Even though the twins fought like cats and dogs most of the time, Alex's illness had reminded both of them how much they really cared about one another. Stevie was sure the same kind of thing would work for Carole and Marie.

Lisa was shaking her head. "I don't know, Stevie—" she began.

Stevie cut her off again. "I've got it!" she exclaimed, dropping her spoon and waving her hands wildly. "Beriberi!"

"What?" Lisa stared at her friend, certain now that Stevie had lost her mind.

"Beriberi," Stevie repeated. "It's a terrible disease." Actually, Stevie didn't know any more about beriberi than that, but she thought it sounded very dramatic. "Let's say Carole just happens to find out that Marie has a fatal case of beriberi, and the only thing that can save her is, hmm, well . . ." Her voice trailed off as she tried to think of something.

"A kidney transplant, maybe?" Lisa suggested sarcastically. "And Carole happens to be the only one with the right blood type?"

"I don't think that will work," Stevie said, not noticing the sarcasm. "It's a little too complicated." Her face brightened again. "I know, we could tell Carole that Marie has to have another operation. It could be something left over from her accident."

"Stevie," Lisa said.

"Or how about this," Stevie went on excitedly. "She could find out she's going to be moving away from Willow

Creek as soon as her mother gets back. We could tell Carole that the real reason Mrs. Dana is in Europe is to look for their new home in Siberia. What do you think?"

"Stevie!" Lisa repeated. "Siberia is in Asia!"

"Whatever. But it still won't work," Stevie answered herself. "Carole would probably be overjoyed to think that Marie was moving far away. It has to be something scarier, like maybe finding out Marie is actually the daughter of a crazed ax murderer—no, a vampire! And he's on his way to claim her as his next victim, and only Carole can stop him. . . ."

By this time Lisa was completely exasperated. "Stevie!" she shouted. "Have you completely lost your mind?"

"What?" Stevie asked, startled out of her plotting. She looked at Lisa. "What's wrong?"

"What's wrong is that your plan is crazy," Lisa said in a quieter voice. "It just won't work. Carole will never fall for any of those silly stories about vampires or beriberi. And we can't put Marie in any real danger."

Something Lisa had just said gave Stevie an idea. "That's it!" she said. "That's a great idea, Lisa. A fall!"

"What?" Lisa had no idea what Stevie was talking about.

"You just said the word 'fall,'" Stevie explained patiently. "That made me think of falling down, which made me think of falling out of the hayloft, which made me think of our sleepover. We can push Marie out of the hayloft during the sleepover."

"What?" Lisa cried, horrified.

"Oh, we'll have a net there to catch her, of course," Stevie added quickly. "We can use that roll of netting that's taking up space in the tack room. I'm sure Max won't mind, especially if we don't tell him until afterward."

Lisa was shaking her head again. "Keep thinking, Stevie," she said with a sigh.

"Well, I guess it couldn't hurt to have a backup plan," Stevie said, but her mind was working full speed ahead on the hayloft idea. She was pretty sure they would be able to hook the netting securely enough so that Marie would be in no danger of hurting herself. And a dramatic fall out of the loft would be sure to scare some sense into Carole. It would work. Stevie was sure of it.

"I CAN'T BELIEVE my English teacher," Carole grumbled the following evening. She and Marie were getting ready to start their homework. Carole's mood hadn't improved much since the day before. If anything, it had gotten worse and worse as she watched Marie and Colonel Hanson talk and joke with each other all through dinner. They both seemed to have forgotten that Carole was still living in the same house with them. At breakfast that morning she'd had to ask for the milk three times before they heard her, because they were laughing so hard at some stupid joke Marie had just told about a dog and a canary. Carole herself hadn't been able to follow it—Marie's rock music had kept her up late again, and she was so exhausted she couldn't think straight. Of course that did nothing to improve Carole's state of mind, not to mention her feelings toward Marie. When she did manage to get a word in edgewise, it was usually snide or sarcastic. She knew she was being grouchy and unpleasant, but she couldn't seem to stop herself, and that made her feel even worse. Now, on top of all that, she had to answer a bunch of discussion questions on *Of Mice and Men*.

"What's wrong, honey?" Colonel Hanson asked, a little distractedly. He and Marie were discussing World War II, the subject of Marie's history assignment and one of Colonel Hanson's favorite topics.

Carole glared at him. He didn't notice, which made her feel even worse. "Never mind," she said. She stomped out of the room and upstairs to her bedroom. When she arrived there, she realized that if she wanted to use the computer to do her homework she'd have to go back down to the living room. "Forget it," she muttered. There was no way she wanted to be in the same room with her father and his newly adopted daughter.

She sat down at her desk, opened her notebook to a fresh page, and picked up a pencil. Chewing on the end, she tried to figure out what to write about. She had been distracted with her plans for Marie's visit when she'd read *Of Mice and Men*, so it hadn't made much of an impression on her—especially since nobody rides a horse anywhere in the book. The questions her teacher had given them didn't even seem to make sense.

She took her copy of the book out of her backpack. Flipping through it aimlessly, she found her thoughts returning to the living room below. Normally she would have asked her father for help with her homework, but that was out of the question now. She was sure he wouldn't be interested even if she did ask. He would much rather discuss World War II with Marie than help his own daughter with her English assignment.

Carole sighed and decided she couldn't possibly concentrate anymore on an empty stomach. She had been in such a bad mood when she arrived home from school that she hadn't even had an afternoon snack. Remembering that there had still been a few of Colonel Hanson's delicious chocolate-chip cookies left over from the day before, she tossed aside her book and pencil and went down to the kitchen.

She poured herself a glass of milk, making a face as she heard the murmur of the lively conversation that was still going on in the other room. She glanced around the kitchen, but the tin of cookies was nowhere to be seen. She checked the oven, the cabinets, and everywhere else she could think of, but they were gone. All she could find was an old bag of store-bought butter cookies. Suddenly she realized where the missing cookies must be: Marie must have eaten them! Carole popped one of the butter cookies into her mouth and chewed angrily. "Ugh. Stale," she muttered.

Gritting her teeth, she stomped out into the living room. Sure enough, the tin that had contained the cookies was sitting on the little table between Marie and Colonel Hanson. But the tin was now empty, except for a few crumbs. As Carole entered, Marie was just popping the last of the cookies into her mouth and washing it down with milk.

Meanwhile, Colonel Hanson was busy telling Marie about the role of the resistance movement within the Third Reich. She was nodding as he spoke, seemingly hanging on every word.

Carole's hands clenched into fists as she watched Marie set down her glass of milk and jot down a note on the paper in front of her. It wasn't fair, Carole thought. Her father was supposed to help her with *her* homework, not some visitor's. And couldn't they at least have saved her one measly cookie?

She cleared her throat loudly. Colonel Hanson and Marie looked up. "Oh, hello, sweetheart," Colonel Hanson said. "Is your homework all done?"

"No," Carole said through clenched teeth. "I haven't even started it yet. I came down to get some cookies, but I see that *somebody* has already eaten them all. I guess that *somebody* never stopped to think that I might like a snack, too. But then, that *somebody* never stops to think at all from what I can tell. She just cracks some stupid joke and does whatever she feels like doing."

Marie's face had been turning redder and redder throughout Carole's speech. Suddenly she burst into tears and ran out of the room. Carole heard the other girl's footsteps thumping up the stairs, and then the sound of a door slamming.

Colonel Hanson stood up, his normally jovial face dark with anger. "Just what was that all about, young lady?" he demanded, his hands on his hips. Before Carole could answer, he held up one hand. "No, I don't want to hear. Whatever your problem is, there's no excuse for taking it out on Marie the way you just did."

"But, Dad, she—" Carole began.

"She nothing," Colonel Hanson interrupted her. "She has done nothing but be a charming, accommodating guest since she arrived on Tuesday. You, on the other hand, have been grouchier and ruder than I've ever seen you. I'm surprised Marie has been able to put up with you this long."

Carole folded her arms across her chest, willing herself not to cry. "Fine. Take her side. As usual."

Colonel Hanson had opened his mouth to say something else, but he closed it again at her words. Then he said, "Her side? Carole, I'm not taking anybody's side here. I'm just pointing out—"

"You're just pointing out everything that's wrong with me and everything that's wonderful about her," Carole said, the words coming in a rush. "I bet you wish Marie were your daughter and that I was the one going home after a couple of weeks."

Colonel Hanson stared at her for a moment. Carole didn't meet his gaze, but instead kept her eyes trained on the ground.

"Is that really what you think?" Colonel Hanson said at last.

Carole shrugged. "Well, what else would I think, after the way you've been swooning over Marie ever since she got here, and ignoring me."

"Carole, are you telling me that you're jealous of the way I've been treating Marie?" Colonel Hanson asked.

Carole just shrugged again.

"You know as well as I do," he went on, "that Marie has been through some tough times lately. And if anyone could understand what she's going through, I thought it would be you. Now, it's obvious that you're upset, and you know I don't like to see that. But this time I think you're just going to have to think things through on your own—calmly and rationally. When you do, I think you'll see how ridiculous you're being, and how poorly you've been treating Marie."

Carole frowned even harder. Part of her mind knew that what her father was saying made sense. But a much louder and angrier part couldn't help thinking that he didn't understand what she was feeling at all. If he did, he would be comforting her, not scolding her.

But she couldn't tell him that, not right now. Not when he was still taking Marie's side. "Fine," she said at last in a tight, cold voice.

Colonel Hanson sighed and nodded. "All right, then," he said. "I'd suggest you go up to your room and stay there. And, Carole, please think about what I've said." With that he turned away from her.

Carole backed out of the room, then turned and ran upstairs to her room. She slammed the door and threw herself facedown onto her bed. The tears of hurt, outrage, and loneliness she had been holding back welled up at last, and she sobbed into her pillow for a long time.

CAROLE MANAGED TO stay out of Marie's way—and her father's—all day Friday. She left early for school in the morning and went up to her room as soon as she got home in the afternoon. At dinner that night Marie and Colonel Hanson hardly seemed to notice Carole's presence as they chatted about Marie's history report, which had gone extremely well, thanks to Colonel Hanson's input. Carole just moved her peas around on her plate as they talked. She had finally finished her English assignment at midnight the night before, but she knew her work wasn't as good as it would have been if she hadn't been so tired and upset while she was writing it.

After dinner, while Colonel Hanson and Marie watched TV in the living room, Carole went up to her room and tried to read a book. She was exhausted from staying up so late the night before, and before long she fell into a deep, dreamless sleep.

She woke up early the next morning, refreshed in body but not in spirit. In fact, she felt more miserable than ever. She wasn't sure she could survive another entire week as Marie's unwilling sister. She was even less certain that she could make it through the hayloft sleepover that night— especially since Stevie and Lisa were sure to make a big fuss over Marie for her birthday. That reminded Carole that she and her father still hadn't gone shopping for Marie's birthday gift. They hadn't even settled on what to get her. Carole found herself hoping spitefully that Colonel Hanson had forgotten all about it—it would serve Marie right. Still, it wasn't likely that the Colonel would forget his favorite new daughter, Carole reminded herself.

Sighing, she sat up in bed and glanced at the clock. It was early, but not too early to head over to Pine Hollow. She really needed someone to talk to, and Starlight was the best listener she knew. He was probably the only one who wouldn't lecture her on how she should be nicer to poor Marie, she thought morosely.

She got up and pulled on her oldest jeans and a flannel shirt. Then she tiptoed out into the hall, pausing a moment to listen. Hearing the sound of gentle snoring coming from her father's bedroom at the end of the hall, and silence from Marie's room, Carole decided with relief that they both must still be asleep.

Moving as quietly as possible, she went downstairs and into the kitchen, where she poured herself a glass of milk. After gulping it down she found some carrots in the vegetable bin in the refrigerator. She stuck them into her pocket for Starlight. Remembering the bag of stale butter cookies, she grabbed that, too.

Last, but not least, she went to the notepad by the phone and scribbled a quick note to her father so he'd know where she was. Then she left the house, grabbed her bike from the garage, and started the long ride to Pine Hollow. The cool morning air felt good against her face. There were no people or cars anywhere in sight, and Carole was glad. She wanted to be alone.

WHEN SHE ARRIVED at Pine Hollow, the stable yard was completely deserted. Inside, the horses had been given their morning feed, but nobody was around. Once again Carole was relieved. She was still in no mood for human companionship. But just being in the presence of all those horses made her feel a little better. On the way to Starlight's stall she stopped to visit some of the others, beginning with Spice, the mare who was supposed to foal soon. Spice greeted her calmly, seeming relaxed and happy in her unfamiliar surroundings. As Carole moved down the aisle, she paused to give a scratch or a pat to each horse she passed.

Starlight's nicker of greeting made Carole feel better than she had in days. "Hi, boy," she said softly, letting herself into the stall. She gave the big gelding a hug, then dug out the treats she'd brought. He crunched happily on the carrots, but after biting down on one of the cookies, he quickly spit it out.

"I don't blame you," Carole told him. "Those cookies aren't good enough for either of us to eat."

Then she set to work grooming him. As she worked, she talked, telling him all about her rotten week with Marie.

"Everyone acts as though I'm the one with the problem," she told the horse. "When, in fact, they're the ones who are acting strange, fussing over Marie like she's the queen of the world."

She finished picking out his hooves and tossed the pick into his grooming bucket. Then she found the body brush and set to work on his gleaming bay hide, paying careful attention to all his special itchy spots. "I mean, just listen to this, Starlight," she continued. "First of all my dad acts like her arrival is the best thing to happen in his whole entire life. He carries her suitcases, fixes her a great snack, and generally acts like she's the funniest person that ever lived.

"Then there's the whole matter of his driving her around everywhere she pleases. Never mind that I usually have to take the bus whenever I want to come here. The bus just isn't good enough for Marie, I guess." Carole paused for breath. Starlight nuzzled her neck, looking for more carrots, and she gave him one.

"And I don't think he would even care if I flunked out of school, as long as Marie's stupid history report gets finished." She paused again for a moment. "Well, actually, come to think of it, he would care. He'd love it if I flunked out, because that would give him another excuse to yell at me."

Starlight moved his head up and down, and Carole would have sworn he was nodding sympathetically. "You see what I have to put up with, boy?" she asked. "It's not just Dad, either. Stevie and Lisa can't stop talking about how wonderful Marie is. They just can't wait to throw her this big party tonight. And they're always laughing at her stupid jokes and saying how funny she is. When she's here, they can't wait to help her tack up and give her private riding lessons—but let me give her one little bit of constructive advice, and they look at me like I'm the big bad wolf."

She traded the body brush for a soft rag. "Do you know how irritating it is when you're the only one who can see how annoying someone else is being? Well, that's just how I feel," she declared. "Even Max is getting in on the act. It's funny how we have to practically beg him to do anything at all around here, and yet when Marie is involved, he just says yes right away, no questions asked."

Carole threw the rag back into the bucket and set to

work combing out Starlight's mane and tail, working out the few tangles expertly but gently. When she was finished, she stepped back and looked at him with satisfaction.

"You're just about the prettiest horse that ever set foot in a barn," she declared. Now that she had vented her frustration about Marie, she felt a little better—although she didn't want to think about what would happen when Marie and Colonel Hanson arrived for the Horse Wise meeting later that morning. She was sure her father would be angry that she had come to the stable without bringing Marie along. Starlight snorted and pawed at the straw with one foreleg. "What's that, boy? You seem a little restless. All right, then, wait here a second. I'll be right back."

She hurried away and returned a moment later with Starlight's bridle and a lunge line. "You obviously could use some exercise, and I've been thinking you need a little lunging practice. We might as well go out and use the ring while no one else is around to bother us." She led him out of the stall and down the wide stable aisle toward the door.

"Wow," said Stevie softly as Starlight's footsteps faded away in the distance. She and Lisa were crouched in the hayloft right above Starlight's stall. They had come over to Pine Hollow early to make sure the loft was clean and ready for the sleepover. By the time they had noticed that Carole was in the stall below them, she had started her one-sided discussion with Starlight. Not wanting to eavesdrop, but not knowing what else to do, the two girls had kept quiet, and so had heard every word.

"Yeah," said Lisa. "Wow is right. We've got to do something."

Stevie nodded. "Then we're in agreement. Let's go see if that netting is still there."

"Wait," Lisa protested. "I'm sure if we keep thinking about it, we can come up with another plan. I just don't think your idea is safe, especially since Marie just finished healing from her last accident."

Stevie looked hurt. "Marie won't get a scratch," she said. "I have everything all planned out. Come on, help me find the net and then I'll show you. It'll be as safe as nursery school."

"Well, you can show me, but I'm not promising anything," Lisa said doubtfully.

They headed for the tack room. The roll of heavyweight netting was in the corner, just as Stevie had remembered. Max had used it as temporary fencing when a storm had knocked down a couple of posts. After the fence was repaired, he had stored it in the tack room, not knowing what else to do with it.

The two girls dragged the roll of netting out into the main section of the barn. Then Stevie put her hands on her hips and looked around, chewing her lower lip thoughtfully. "Let's see, now, we just have to figure out how to attach it. . . ." she said.

Lisa groaned. "Stevie, I can't believe you're really serious about this. You've had some crazy schemes before, but this one just about takes the cake."

"Come on, Lisa," Stevie said. "You heard Carole just now. Desperate times call for desperate measures." She couldn't quite remember where she'd heard that phrase, but she liked the way it sounded. "This will work, you'll see. During that split second when Carole actually believes Marie is falling, she'll realize just how much she likes her. It'll be perfect!"

"Oh, yeah?" Lisa said darkly. "Then what happens afterward, when Carole—not to mention Marie—realizes she's been tricked?"

Stevie grinned. "We can't let a little detail like that stop us."

"Right," Lisa muttered. "Because once Carole figures out what we did, she's going to throw us down after Marie!"

"Horse Wise, come to order!"

At Max's words the members of Pine Hollow's Pony Club immediately quieted down and turned toward him expectantly. It was ten o'clock and time for the weekly Saturday-morning meeting to begin. Everyone was seated in a wide circle in the indoor ring. Horse Wise alternated between mounted and unmounted meetings, and this week's was unmounted. Pony Club members were supposed to learn all about horse care—not just riding, but also things like grooming, stable management, and even veterinary care. Max often invited special speakers to come and talk to the Horse Wise members during the unmounted meetings. Judy Barker had spoken to the group many times, as had the local farrier and other experts in various fields.

Today, however, there was no speaker scheduled. Max stood in the center of the circle and waited until he was sure he had the undivided attention of everyone in the room—which included parent volunteers as well as young riders.

"Good morning, everyone," he began. "Today we have a special guest sitting in on our meeting." He held out his hand to where Marie was sitting between Colonel Hanson and Stevie. "Marie Dana is staying with the Hansons for a little while," Max continued, "and therefore she is welcome here. Especially since today happens to be her birthday."

A chorus of greetings and "happy birthdays" rose from the group. Most of the people present had met Marie before. Marie smiled and gave a little wave in reply. Carole, who was sitting on the other side of Stevie, scowled.

"Now," Max went on, "on the agenda for today is something we haven't done in quite a while: a pop-quiz mini-know-down."

Carole perked up a little at that. A know-down was a type of quiz game that tested players' knowledge of all kinds of horse facts. It worked sort of like a spelling bee, except that each player could choose the difficulty level of his or her question. Sometimes Max gave members time to study. But occasionally he would have them play a short game without warning. As he said, it was like a pop quiz in school, and it was useful for the same reason. It gave players a chance to prove that they were learning all the time, not just studying for a specific game.

Because she knew more about horses than almost anyone else in Horse Wise, Carole was very good at the game. Normally she didn't go out of her way to show off, but this time she thought she just might. After all, it was time she got a little positive attention. Maybe if she won the game, it would show her father that she could do something right, after all.

"All right, let's begin," Max was saying. "You're first, May. What level question do you want?"

May Grover, a beginning rider who was a few years younger than the Saddle Club girls, thought for a second. "I'll take a two-point question, Max," she said.

Max nodded. "All right." He glanced at the list of questions in his hand. "Name at least two things that can give a horse saddle sores."

May thought for a second. "His saddle might not fit right," she said. "Or it might be dirty."

Max nodded. "Good. Two points."

Meg Durham, a member who was about the same age as the Saddle Club girls, was next. "I'll try a three-pointer, Max," she decided.

"How can a horse best see objects that are very far away or very close to him, and why is this so?" Max asked.

"Um . . . by turning his head?" Meg said uncertainly. "Because his eyes are on the side of his head?"

"Sorry," said Max. "Betsy, the question goes to you."

Betsy Cavanaugh cleared her throat. "To see something far away, the horse would hold its head high," she said. "To see something close, it would lower its head. And I think it is because of the way horses' eyes are positioned—they don't have very good depth perception."

Max nodded. "Good. Three points."

Carole nodded, too. She had known the answer—in fact, she didn't really think the question was worth three points. She was a little surprised that Meg had missed it.

Max continued around the circle. Before long it was Lisa's turn. She came up with the correct answer to a two-point question about leg bandaging. Carole was next.

"Four points, please," she said confidently.

Max nodded. "Here's a tough one, then. Name the three stallions from whom every modern Thoroughbred is descended."

Carole thought for a second. "The Darley Arabian and the Godolphin Arabian are two of them," she said. For a second she couldn't remember the third name. "Oh, and the Byerly Turk," she finally recalled.

"Excellent," Max said.

Lisa looked at Carole with respect. "I didn't even know what Max was talking about," she whispered. "Congratulations."

Carole smiled, feeling proud of herself. She knew that it would have been a difficult question for most of the people in the room to answer. However, Carole liked to read everything she could about horses, and she had recently finished a book about the three legendary sires who had founded the Thoroughbred breed. It wasn't a fact that would make anyone at Pine Hollow a better rider, but it was an important point in equestrian history, and Carole thought the fact that she'd known the answer showed the depth of her knowledge.

Stevie got her question right, too, and then it was Marie's turn. "How about it, Marie?" Max said. "I hope you'll play our little game."

"Sure, I'll give it a shot," Marie said with a shrug. "But I'd better stick to a one-pointer."

"Okay," Max said. "What is a 'hand'?"

"Hey, I know this one—it's four inches, right?" Marie answered. "It's how you measure a horse's height."

Max smiled. "Excellent! That's exactly right."

Colonel Hanson gave Marie a pat on the back. "Good show, Marie," he said.

Stevie, Lisa, and some of the others congratulated Marie as well.

"Thanks, everyone" Marie said with a grin. "It must be because of my birthday. I'm not only getting older, I'm getting smarter."

Everyone laughed except Carole, who just rolled her eyes. It figured. Nobody except Max and Lisa had even bothered to comment on the difficult question Carole had answered, but here everyone was congratulating Marie as if she'd just told them the meaning of life.

The next time around Marie was braver. "I'll try a two-pointer this time," she told Max.

"Okay," he said. He glanced down at the list. "What are the bars?"

Marie shrugged. It was obvious that she had no idea. "Someplace a horse goes for a drink?" she guessed with a grin. Several people chuckled at the joke.

"That's wrong," Carole called out, forgetting for a moment that the question should go to the next person in line, who happened to be Adam Levine. "They're the sensitive toothless gums in a horse's mouth. The bit goes over them."

"Thank you, Carole," Max said, looking displeased. "You just earned two points for Adam. Please remember to answer only when it's your turn."

Carole sat back and stared at the ground, her face flaming, as giggles erupted from other players. She glanced at Marie out of the corner of her eye, but Marie wasn't one of the gigglers. In fact, her face was red, too, and she was staring at the ground just like Carole.

After a few more rounds Carole was so far ahead of the others that Max declared her the winner, ending the game. She had taken a four-point question every time and gotten all of them right.

"Nice work, Carole," Max told her. "I hope everyone

has learned something new today. That's it for our Horse Wise meeting; those of you who are in the flat class, go get tacked up and meet me in the outdoor ring in fifteen minutes."

Stevie, Lisa, and Carole were all in the flat class, as well as the jump class that followed it.

"Marie, you're going to join the class, aren't you?" said Stevie. She glanced at Carole out of the corner of her eye as she said it. Carole had been acting so unpredictably lately—Stevie was afraid she'd get her head bitten off for even talking to Marie. Then Stevie immediately felt guilty for having such thoughts. She wasn't going to be mean to Marie just to make Carole happy, but Carole was her friend and she was obviously miserable. Stevie couldn't help feeling sorry for her, especially since she knew what it was like to be in the grips of an extreme case of sibling rivalry.

In any case, Carole didn't seem to be listening to Stevie or anyone else. She appeared to be lost in thoughts of her own, her face set in its now-familiar frown.

"Sure," Marie said in answer to Stevie's question. "Max said it would be okay to take the flat class. He's not even going to charge me for it—it's his birthday gift to me." Her words were light, but Stevie couldn't help noticing that her tone was softer and more serious than usual.

"Great," Stevie replied. "Come on, I'll help you tack up." She threw one more worried glance at Carole before following Marie toward the tack room.

Fifteen minutes later the flat class began. For most of the class time Max had the students work on posting and sitting trots. Even though they were good things for riders of all levels to practice, Carole couldn't help wondering if Max was taking it easy that day because of Marie. Still, she was glad to notice that he barked orders at Marie just as if she were a regular member of the class.

The jump class began as soon as the flat class ended. The riders who weren't taking the jump class, including Marie, headed inside to untack their horses. If Max had been taking it easy during the flat class, he seemed determined to make up for it now. For the next hour Carole was too busy to think about Marie at all.

"THAT WAS A great class," Lisa commented as she, Stevie, and Carole led their horses inside after the class had ended.

Carole nodded. The jump class had improved her mood immensely—she realized it was the first time all week that she had really concentrated on something other than Marie Dana. Reminded of her houseguest, Carole looked around, expecting to see Marie hanging around somewhere waiting for them. But she was nowhere in sight.

"Hey, where's Marie?" said Stevie, as if reading Carole's mind.

"I don't know," said Carole. "Maybe she went home." She couldn't help hoping she was right. The girls had planned to stay at Pine Hollow all day—Carole's father was supposed to come back later with their sleeping bags and suitcases for the sleepover. Maybe Marie had forgotten all about their plans. Still, Carole knew that her father would have a fit if she didn't try to track her down.

So after Starlight was comfortably settled in his stall, Carole called home. Her father answered.

"Hi, Dad," Carole said shyly. She hadn't really spoken to her father much since Thursday night. It was the longest she'd ever stayed angry with him, and it felt strange and unpleasant.

"Carole?" Colonel Hanson said. "Is anything wrong?"

"I don't think so," Carole replied. "I just wanted to check to make sure Marie is there with you."

"Marie?" repeated Colonel Hanson, obviously confused. "But she's at Pine Hollow with you."

"No, she isn't," Carole said. "I thought she went home after the flat class."

"She isn't here," Colonel Hanson replied. He sounded worried.

Suddenly Carole was feeling worried, too. If Marie wasn't at home and she wasn't at Pine Hollow, where was she?

"Well, she must be around here someplace," Carole said, trying to sound reassuring. "I'm sure I just missed her."

"Do you think so?" Colonel Hanson didn't sound convinced. "Well, call me back if you don't find her soon."

"I promise." Carole hung up and went to find Lisa and

Stevie. They also seemed to have disappeared, although Carole wasn't really worried about them. She just wished they were there to help her search for Marie.

Carole sat down to think. Where would Marie go? She tried to put herself in the other girl's place.

As she did, she slowly began to realize why Marie must have disappeared. Carole had spent so much time that day trying to avoid Marie that she hadn't stopped to think that Marie might also be trying to avoid *her*. After all, she'd been pretty mean to her for the past few days. Why would Marie want to spend her birthday with someone who couldn't speak to her without snarling?

Carole had the sinking feeling that Marie had probably disappeared to nurse a set of very hurt feelings. And she also suspected she knew where Marie might have disappeared *to*.

"Sorry, boy," she told Starlight as she slipped on his bridle a moment later. "I know you earned your rest for today, but I just need you to take me one more place." She stuck a lead rope in her pocket, then led the horse to the mounting block and climbed onto his bare back. "I just hope Max doesn't see us riding out by ourselves," she muttered, more to herself than to the horse. Then she put that thought out of her mind. She didn't have time to worry about Max right now. She gave Starlight a nudge with her heel, and he obediently set off across the fields behind Pine Hollow.

When Carole and Starlight reached the Danas' house, which was just a few minutes' ride from the stable, it appeared to be silent and deserted. Carole slid off Starlight's back and clipped the lead to his bridle. After securing him to a nearby tree branch, she walked up to the house's front door and tried the handle. Locked.

She walked around to the back of the house. The back door was locked, too. But as Carole was turning away, she thought she heard a noise coming from the side of the house.

She walked quietly around the corner of the house and saw a small garden shed in the side yard. The sound seemed to be coming from the shed. And it sounded like someone crying.

"Marie?" Carole called softly.

The crying sound stopped immediately.

"Who is it?" Marie's voice called suspiciously.

Carole breathed a sigh of relief. She had been right. Marie had come to the most comforting place she could be right now—home. "It's me—Carole," Carole said, opening the door to the little shed.

Marie was inside, her face wet with tears. She was frowning. "What do *you* want?" she demanded angrily. "Did you track me down so you could yell at me and humiliate me some more?"

Carole looked at the ground. "I guess I deserve that," she said. And she meant it. She'd been mean and spiteful

112

toward Marie all week. Somehow, despite all her good intentions at the beginning of Marie's visit, Carole had ended up doing more harm than good. Marie must be feeling terribly lonely and hurt right now, and it was all Carole's fault.

Carole gulped. "Marie," she began hesitantly, "I think I owe you a big apology. I mean a *really* big apology."

Marie looked wary as she swiped her tearstained face with one sleeve, then folded her arms across her chest. "I'm listening," she said coldly.

"I guess I haven't been seeing your point of view this whole week," Carole said. "I've been so busy being jealous of all the attention you were getting that I forgot what it's like to be in your situation. I couldn't understand why my father was treating you better than he was treating me."

"Jealous?" Marie repeated. "You were jealous of me?" She seemed honestly surprised. "But your dad is crazy about you. How could you think those things?"

Carole shrugged. "I don't know," she said. "It was mostly stupid little things that made me crazy, like the two of you eating those cookies."

Marie almost smiled. "Yeah. You seemed pretty upset about that," she said. "You must have been really hungry."

"Hungry for attention, I guess," Carole admitted. "The funny thing is, I've always wanted a sister or brother, but now that I've actually had the chance to have one, I've realized that I'm just not used to sharing my dad with anyone. Apparently I'm not very good at it."

"Well," Marie said thoughtfully, "I guess I wasn't really going out of my way to look at things from your point of view, either. I was pretty busy worrying about how I'd be able to deal with my mom's being gone and all. So I didn't stop to think about how you'd have to deal with having me in your house."

Carole took a deep breath and gave Marie a tentative smile. "Well, I'm willing to try to do better from now on if you are. How about it?"

"Deal," Marie said. She stuck out her hand.

Carole shook it, feeling a little awkward. "Oh, by the way, happy birthday."

"Thanks," Marie replied.

Carole bit her lip. "I'm really sorry, Marie," she said quietly. "About everything."

Marie pulled her hand back and swiped at her eyes again. "Yeah. Me, too." She cleared her throat. "I'm glad you found me."

Carole nodded. "Same here. I had a feeling you'd be here. I figured you'd want to be at home at a time like this."

"Actually, that's not the only reason I came home," Marie said. "I was hoping to be able to get into my house and get my portable CD player and some disks. Not that I don't appreciate the loan of your radio, but it's just not the same, you know?" She laughed. "Anyway, I figured that if you were going to be mean to me for the rest of the week, at least I'd be able to turn up the volume in my headphones and drown you out."

"Very funny," Carole said dryly. She wasn't sure if she was glad or sorry to see that Marie's sense of humor was back. Still, she had to laugh a little in spite of herself. "I guess you didn't find a way in?"

Marie shook her head sadly. "Everything's locked on the first floor. I'm pretty sure the second-floor hall window is open, but the only way to get to it is that trellis, and I couldn't reach it." She pointed to an empty wooden trellis attached to the side of the house nearby.

Carole glanced at the trellis. Suddenly she had an idea. "Marie, I think I feel a bout of Stevie-ism coming on," she said slowly.

"What?" said Marie.

"Wait here a minute," Carole replied mysteriously. "I'll be right back."

A moment later she returned, leading Starlight.

"Are you going to have him kick the door in, or what?" asked Marie, mystified.

"Give me a leg up, will you?" was Carole's only reply. Marie obeyed. "Now lead him over to the trellis and hold him still," Carole directed.

Comprehension dawned on Marie's face. She smiled and did as Carole ordered.

115

When Starlight was in place and standing quietly, Carole slowly and carefully adjusted her position until she was standing upright on his broad, bare back. She reached up and grabbed the trellis, then pulled herself up hand over hand until she could get a foothold.

Seconds later she reached the window. Trying it, she found that it was unlocked just as Marie had thought. Carole climbed through and then looked down at Marie. "Tie Starlight up and come around front," she called.

Marie nodded. Carole made her way through the house and down the stairs and let Marie in the front door. They went back upstairs together. Marie quickly collected her small portable CD player and a few disks and threw them in her backpack. The girls locked the window, then left the house again through the front door which locked behind them. Carole helped Marie climb up behind her on Starlight, and they headed back to Pine Hollow together.

MAX WAS WAITING for them when they arrived. "Carole, your father has called three times in the last half hour," he said, shaking his head. "You'd better give him a ring to let him know you're both alive and well." He reached for Starlight's bridle as the girls dismounted. "You can use the office phone. Meantime I'll put this fellow in his stall for you." He began to lead Starlight away, then stopped and turned. "And by the way, you're forgiven for breaking the

116

no-riding-alone rule," he added gruffly. "But just this once."

"Thanks, Max," Carole said gratefully. "I'll never do it again, I promise. Oh, and I'll be back to groom Starlight in a few minutes."

Max nodded and ambled off with Starlight in tow.

"I'll call your father," Marie said. "I want to apologize for scaring him. I shouldn't have just taken off like that without telling anyone."

Carole followed her to the office. After Marie had made her apologies to Colonel Hanson, she listened for a moment. Then she put her hand over the receiver. "He says he wants to take us both out for a big birthday dinner before the sleepover," she told Carole. "Then we can pick up our pajamas and stuff and he'll drive us back here in time to meet Stevie and Lisa at eight o'clock."

Carole smiled. "He's probably plotting ways to get us to be nice to each other," she said. "Maybe he thought a restaurant meal would put us in a friendlier mood. Here, let me talk to him." She took the receiver. "Hi, Dad? It's me."

"Carole?" her father said. "Did Marie tell you about the dinner plans?"

"Yes," Carole replied. "And I wanted to tell you, Marie and I don't need to go out to dinner together."

"Carole!" Colonel Hanson began, sounding angry. "I had hoped you'd . . ."

"No, no, it's not that," Carole interrupted him with a

laugh. "What I meant was that Marie and I are friends again. I apologized for being such a rotten hostess all week." She caught Marie's eye. "And such a rotten friend. So you don't need to try to make us like each other anymore. We took care of that ourselves."

Colonel Hanson chuckled. "Boy, am I glad to hear that," he said. "But still, that's all the more reason for me to take you girls out. What better way to celebrate friendship than with a nice dinner? Besides, it's still Marie's birthday. Don't you want to give her our present?"

"Our present?" Carole repeated, suddenly remembering that they'd never followed through on their plans to go shopping. "But we didn't get her anything yet." She glanced in Marie's direction.

"Oh, yes, we did," Colonel Hanson corrected her. "It's just going to be a surprise for you as well as for her. And I know how you love a good surprise."

"I guess I can't argue with that," Carole said with a smile. "When are you picking us up?"

12

"OKAY, THE NET'S secure," Stevie announced, climbing the ladder to the hayloft, where Lisa was busy arranging their sleeping bags. "All we have to do when we're ready is stretch it across and attach it to the hooks in the far wall."

Lisa rolled her eyes. "I don't think you quite understood me when I told you there was no way I was going to be a part of this idiotic scheme of yours, Stevie," she said.

"Don't worry. It's foolproof," Stevie assured her briskly. She sat down on a bale of hay and rubbed her hands together eagerly. "Now, let's go over our parts one more time. First I'll distract Carole and Marie with a demonstration of my special shadow puppets." She switched on the battery-operated lamp Max had lent them to make sure it was working. It was.

Lisa just sighed and shook her head.

"Then," Stevie went on, "you'll sneak down and hook up the net. When you get back, it'll be time to suggest we do some square dancing."

Lisa raised her eyebrows. "Did you say square dancing?" she asked incredulously. "Why would we want to do that?"

"Well, we're in a barn," Stevie said, as if that were the most logical thing in the world. She pointed to her portable tape player. "I have the square-dance tape all cued up. Anyway, when we get to the part about 'swing your partners,' well . . ."

Lisa groaned. "I can't believe I'm sitting here listening to this," she said. "You really think we're going to do this, don't you?"

Stevie looked hurt. "Of course. It's the only way to get Carole and Marie to be friends again."

"It's—" Whatever Lisa had been about to say was cut off as Carole's head popped over the edge of the loft.

"Hi there, you guys," she said cheerfully. "Sorry we're late."

"No problem," Stevie said, jumping to her feet. "Come on up, and let's get this sleepover on the road!"

Carole climbed up into the loft, followed by Marie. "So what's that fence netting doing hanging on the wall down there?" Carole asked.

Stevie gulped. "Uh, what netting would that be?" she asked.

Carole gave her a strange look. "Don't tell me you didn't see it."

Stevie shrugged. "I didn't see a thing. Did you, Lisa?"

Lisa just rolled her eyes again and didn't answer.

"I have a feeling these two have something to hide," Marie said to Carole.

Carole nodded. "I think you're right. Should we try to bribe them into telling us with the leftover birthday cake we brought from the restaurant?"

"Nah," said Marie. "Let's just toss them over the side and eat it all ourselves."

Lisa and Stevie gasped simultaneously.

"Aha!" said Marie. "That got a reaction. It must be a clue!"

"But what could it mean?" Carole said. "Were they planning to ambush us and steal our cake, maybe toss us off the loft during the night?" She glanced at Stevie and noticed the guilty look on her face. "Hey, what *were* you guys planning, anyway?" she asked, dropping the joking tone. "Lisa?"

Lisa glared at Stevie. "Well, it certainly wasn't my idea."

Stevie gave Carole and Marie a weak grin. "I'm just glad to see that you two are getting along better," she said.

"That's right," Carole said. "That means the two of us will gang up on you and tickle you to death if you don't tell us what's going on." She curled her fingers threateningly.

"Well," Stevie began reluctantly, "we were trying to

think of a way to get you two to be friendlier. It's been a little tense around here this week, you know."

"Fair enough," Carole said, and Marie nodded.

"So we tried to think of a plan," Stevie continued.

"You mean *you* tried to think of a plan," Lisa muttered.

"We decided the best way to get you to make up would be to make you, Carole, think Marie was in deadly danger," Stevie said all in one breath. "Then you'd realize how much you really liked her while you were trying to save her life. We were going to push her out of the loft."

"What?" Marie squawked.

"Don't worry," Stevie hurried to add. "That's what the net was for."

"Are you out of your mind?" Carole demanded.

"That's what I said," Lisa told her, nodding.

"How exactly were you planning to do this?" Marie asked.

Stevie bit her lip. "Well, we were going to do it while we were square-dancing," she explained.

"Square-dancing?" Carole and Marie said in unison. They stared at Stevie for a moment, then turned and stared at each other. Then they both burst out laughing. After a moment Lisa joined in. Stevie started to smile, then chuckle, and soon all four girls were rolling with laughter.

"Oh, wow," Carole gasped when she was able to speak again. "We must have really been making things uncomfortable if you were willing to risk life and limb—Marie's, that is—to fix things up between us!"

Stevie grinned sheepishly. "Well, you weren't exactly a barrel of laughs to be around," she said. "You were both obviously miserable. We had to do something."

Carole smiled. "I guess that's what friends are for. But don't worry, I've learned my lesson—even without the square dancing."

Meanwhile, Marie had crawled over to the edge of the loft and was peering down. "Hey, you guys," she called. "I have an idea."

"I hope it's better than Stevie's," Lisa commented. Stevie threw a handful of straw at her.

"Well, actually, it's inspired by Stevie's idea," Marie said.

Carole groaned. "Uh-oh, we're in trouble."

"No, listen," Marie said. "If it was going to be okay to throw me into the net—"

"Well, actually, we hadn't exactly determined that yet," Lisa interrupted.

"Well, all right," said Marie, "since it was *probably* going to be okay to throw me into the net, why don't we get a whole big pile of hay and jump down into it from up here?"

"That's a great idea!" Stevie exclaimed. She hurried to the edge and looked over. Then she glanced around the loft. "We can push a bunch of these bales over. It'll be fun!"

The others couldn't help but agree. They set to work making a soft mountain of hay on the stable floor. When they had enough, they took turns leaping off the edge of the loft into the pillowy pile.

"This is even more fun than jumping into a big pile of leaves," Stevie declared as she scrambled up the ladder, ready for another turn.

"I'd even say it's more fun than square dancing," Marie said mischievously.

"Definitely," Carole said with a laugh. She stepped to the edge and jumped. She landed on her back and looked up at the others with a contented smile. "And it smells sweeter than anything else in the world."

"Enough talking!" Marie said. "Hurry up and move if you don't want me falling on top of you."

After a while, exhausted, the girls stopped jumping. They sat in a row on the edge of the loft, looking down at the hay pile. By now the pile had lost most of its shape. In fact, bits and pieces of it were scattered all over the floor. "I just have one question," Lisa said.

"What's that?" asked Stevie.

"How are we going to explain this to Max?"

"Uh-oh," said Carole. "I hadn't thought of that." She smiled. "But then again, anyone who could come up with something as dumb as the idea of square-dancing out of a hayloft should certainly be able to explain a simple little misplaced mountain of hay."

Before Stevie could answer, the girls heard the stable door slide open.

"Yoo-hoo, anybody home?" called a familiar voice.

The four girls stared at each other. "Max!" they gasped in a single voice.

A second later Max and Deborah came into view. The first thing they did was stare at the huge pile of hay. The second thing they did was burst into laughter.

The girls looked at each other again, this time in puzzlement. "What's so funny?" Stevie called down.

Max looked up at them, still chuckling. "What's funny is that I was just this minute telling Deborah that Red and I were going to spend tomorrow morning bringing down a whole load of hay from the loft." He waved a hand at the hay mountain. "But look at this! The hay fairies were here before us." He winked at Deborah.

"We do what we can," Stevie said graciously. Carole and Lisa glanced at each other, relieved that Max wasn't angry. "So where are you two lovebirds off to now?" Stevie added.

"We're going out for a late dinner," Deborah said. "So I guess you girls are in charge here for a few hours."

Max groaned. "Hush. Just the thought of that gives me indigestion." He looked up at the girls. "Try not to get into too much trouble while we're gone."

"Right," Stevie whispered loudly as Max and Deborah headed for the door. "Like he believes that!"

After the adults were gone, Stevie grabbed her backpack

and held it behind her back. "And now," she announced dramatically, "it's birthday-party time!" With a flourish she pulled out the CD, which Lisa had wrapped in red-and-green paper.

"The paper's left over from last Christmas," she explained to Marie sheepishly. "I hope you don't mind."

"Hey, no problem," Marie said. "I can't believe you guys got me a gift at all. This is great." She eagerly ripped open the package and squealed with delight. "Wow! I can't believe this! I was already plotting ways to make my mom buy this album for me when she got back. I can't wait to listen to it. Thanks a million, you guys!" She reached for her suitcase. "Hey, do you want to see what Carole and her dad got me?"

"Well, my dad was the one who actually got it," Carole admitted. "He went shopping yesterday on his lunch hour."

"But he did say you were the one who gave him the idea," Marie said. "And somehow I believe him."

When she pulled out the gift, Lisa and Stevie started laughing. They knew exactly what Marie meant. The gift was a small leather CD carrying case with a picture of a running horse embossed on it. "It does look like something Carole would pick out. I can't quite put my finger on why, though," Lisa teased.

Carole laughed, too. It felt good to joke around with her

friends again after being in such a bad mood all week. "I saw one like it at the mall last time Dad and I were there," she explained. "I thought about saving up to get it for you for Christmas, Stevie, except they only had ones to hold CDs, not tapes. But I thought it would be perfect for Marie. Now she can bring her CDs with her wherever she goes without worrying about their getting damaged."

"It really is the perfect gift," Stevie declared as Marie carefully tucked her new CD into her new CD case. And the others couldn't help but agree—especially Carole.

Later that night, after the girls had told ghost stories, talked about horses, gossiped about people they knew, talked about horses, eaten the snacks they had brought, talked about horses, and said good night to all the horses in the barn, they were finally ready to settle down and go to sleep.

"This is the life," Stevie commented as the four girls once again sat at the edge of the loft, this time in their pajamas, watching the horses in the stalls below.

"You're not kidding," Marie agreed.

Carole smiled. After all the anger and frustration she'd felt over the past week, it felt good just to relax and be herself again. She looked down at Topside, whose stall was just below where she was sitting, and at the mare Spice, who was nearby in the foaling stall. If she stood up, she would be able to see Starlight, but she was too sleepy to make the effort. It was enough just to know that he was there.

"Well, I don't know about the rest of you, but I'm exhausted," Stevie said a few minutes later. "Let's hit the hay." She grinned, pleased with her unintentional but very appropriate joke. "Literally, that is!"

Lisa had set up their sleeping bags on a soft bed of hay and straw. Naturally, the girls continued to talk even after they'd climbed into their sleeping bags, but gradually they all grew quiet, listening to the sweet, comforting sounds of the horses below. One by one, they dropped off to sleep.

CAROLE AWOKE WITH a start. Someone was shaking her shoulder and whispering her name. It was chilly, and bright moonlight poured over her. For a second Carole couldn't remember where she was. Then she heard a soft whinny from below, and then an answering snort, and she remembered: She was in the stable loft.

"Carole," Marie whispered again insistently.

"What is it?" Carole whispered back. "I'm awake."

"Come see," Marie replied.

Carole followed her as she crawled to the edge of the loft. Marie pointed down. "Look at that!" she said softly, her voice full of wonder.

Carole soon saw why. There in the foaling stall, illuminated by moonlight, was the mare Spice—and a spindly-legged little foal. "Oh!" gasped Carole, delighted.

"I can't believe it's standing up already," Marie marveled.

Carole nodded, watching the pair below carefully. "She must have foaled a while ago—I'd guess it's been at least an hour. Look, the foal is trying to nurse." The girls watched, breathless, as the foal nuzzled its mother's belly in search of food. They could tell when it found it, for the tiny horse let out a squeal of excitement before settling down to nursing vigorously.

"Hey, what time is it?" Marie whispered suddenly.

Carole glanced at her watch, squinting to make out the time in the moonlight. "About five minutes to midnight. Why?"

Marie smiled and glanced down at the foal. "That means he was born on my birthday," she said.

Carole smiled, too. "That's wonderful, Marie," she said. "It's like an extra present."

Marie nodded. "It's a nice one, too," she said quietly. She paused. "This has been kind of a strange birthday, you know?"

"I know," Carole replied. She was sure Marie was thinking about her father. "It was hard for me the first few holidays, too. It still is, really."

Marie nodded sadly. "It just seems weird to be celebrating something like a birthday, when . . ." Her voice trailed off.

"I know," Carole said again. "But your dad would want

you to have a nice birthday. Who knows, he may be looking down at you right now. Maybe he even had something to do with the foal being born tonight—you know, like his gift to you."

Carole regretted her words as soon as she said them. She bit her lip, expecting Marie to get upset at her comment, or at least to make fun of it. But Marie did neither. Instead she leaned over to give Carole a hug.

"Thanks," Marie said. In the silvery light Carole could see tears glistening in the other girl's eyes, but she had a feeling they weren't really tears of sadness—at least not entirely.

"Happy birthday," Carole whispered again as she hugged her back.

Marie sat back, and they watched the moonlit stall below for a few minutes in silence. Then Marie crawled back to wake Stevie and Lisa.

"What's going on?" Stevie murmured sleepily a moment later.

"Oh! She foaled!" whispered Lisa, peering downward.

They all watched the little family in silence. It was obvious that the mare had everything under control and didn't require any human intervention. In fact, she seemed totally unaware of the observers above her as she nuzzled her baby lovingly.

Soon, despite their fascination, the girls started yawning.

By this time the foal had finished nursing and had lain down in the straw to sleep. Reluctantly, the girls tore themselves away from the magical scene below and did the same thing. And the rest of the night was filled with sweet dreams for all of them.

A WEEK LATER Stevie, Carole, and Lisa were sitting in their favorite booth at TD's having a Saddle Club meeting.

"I bet Marie was glad to see her mother," Lisa said, taking a sip of water.

Carole nodded. "You should have seen her at the airport last night. When they announced that the plane was going to be half an hour late, she wanted to sue the airline. And when the plane finally arrived, she jumped up and down the whole time it was landing."

Stevie and Lisa laughed.

"That sounds like Marie," Lisa commented. The girls paused to thank the waitress as she brought them their two hot-fudge sundaes and one blueberry on butter brickle.

"Yeah," Carole said as she dug in. "You know, I can't

believe I'm saying this, but I'm kind of going to miss having her around." She rolled her eyes. "Even if she did play that stupid CD you two gave her twenty-four hours a day for the past week."

"Spoken like a true sister!" Lisa declared.

"Not like *this* sister," Stevie corrected. "I never miss my brothers when they're not around."

"Oh, but that's brothers. Having a sister must be different," Lisa said.

"It's different, all right," Carole said. "A *lot* different from what I was expecting."

"Really?" asked Stevie.

Carole nodded. "I really like Marie—I always have. And I hope she'll be my friend for a long time to come." She shook her head. "But no matter how much I like her, it's tougher being her sister than I would have thought."

"Well, that's probably because being sisters is a much different kind of relationship," Lisa said. "It's more difficult because you each have more adjusting to do."

"That's for sure," Carole agreed. "I never realized how much adjusting people have to do to one another."

"Like Max and Deborah," Stevie pointed out. "Now that they're getting married, he goes shopping for china and she lets him open doors for her."

"Right," Lisa said, nodding thoughtfully. "Those are minor adjustments that make their life together smoother. They want to be together, so they both adjust."

133

But Stevie had been distracted by the entrance of two customers. "Will you look at that," she exclaimed.

Carole and Lisa turned to look. "Oh, great, it's Veronica," Carole said with a shrug. Then her eyes widened. "Isn't that your buddy Priscilla with her?"

Stevie nodded, watching as Priscilla Tyler and Veronica diAngelo sat down at a table on the other side of the restaurant. The two girls didn't notice The Saddle Club watching them—they were chattering animatedly, pausing once in a while to look down at their feet with interest.

"My guess is that there's an intense shoe discussion going on at their table," Lisa remarked.

"My guess is that you're right," Carole agreed.

"That just proves that sometimes the adjusting just isn't worth it," Stevie said, returning to their previous conversation. "Like with me and Priscilla. If we'd wanted to hang out together, one or both of us would have had to undergo a total personality transplant."

"Well, luckily she seems to have found a soul mate," Carole said with a laugh.

"Adjusting to Marie was worth it, though, wasn't it?" Lisa asked Carole.

"Sure," she agreed. "Underneath it all Marie and I really have a lot in common—a lot more than Stevie and Priscilla do, for instance. And I think we both learned a lot from each other. Once we got adjusted to being sisters, it was really kind of fun to have her around."

134

"That's just one more thing I like about The Saddle Club," said Stevie contentedly.

"What is?" asked Lisa.

"We don't have to adjust to one another," Stevie explained. "We're just each who we are and that's fine with all of us."

"Right, like when one of us comes up with some wild notion about throwing somebody out of a hayloft into a net?" Carole asked.

"Well, but you see, I always knew that Lisa would never let me go through with that," Stevie explained. "That's why you two are my best friends—so I don't get into a lot of trouble."

"A lot *more* trouble, you mean," Carole corrected her.

Stevie grinned. "Right! And that's what best friends are for!"

ABOUT THE AUTHOR

BONNIE BRYANT is the author of more than a hundred books about horses, including The Saddle Club series, Saddle Club Super Editions, the Pony Tails series, and Pine Hollow, which follows the Saddle Club girls into their teens. She has also written novels and movie novelizations under her married name, B. B. Hiller.

Ms. Bryant began writing The Saddle Club in 1986. Although she had done some riding before that, she intensified her studies then and found herself learning right along with her characters Stevie, Carole, and Lisa. She claims that they are all much better riders than she is.

Ms. Bryant was born and raised in New York City. She still lives there, in Greenwich Village, with her two sons.